Antoine scanned th

He recognized Geraldi photograph, though sh expected. Her fair hair were wide and almost navy blue and her mouth was a perfect Cupid's bow. She was dressed casually and looked very English.

She only had one suitcase, which surprised him. It wasn't much for a six-month stay.

He took a deep breath, holding up a hand in greeting.

She smiled when she saw him. *"Bonjour, Monsieur et…"* She trailed off before rallying with *"Merci beaucoup pour me recevoir chez vous."*

He hadn't expected her to speak in French and appreciated the effort. *"De rien."* He paused. Was she *Mademoiselle* or *Madame*? Not wanting to get it wrong, he switched to English. "You're very welcome, Dr. Milligan."

"Geri, please." She held out her hand.

"Antoine." He shook her hand and felt as if he'd been galvanized. He'd never reacted to anyone like that before, even Céline, and it threw him. "I wasn't sure how much luggage you'd have," he said, dropping her hand and hoping that she couldn't tell how much she'd flustered him.

Dear Reader,

I love Paris, so when my editor suggested that I write a vet book, I asked if I could set it in Paris. And I couldn't resist including the panda babies; my husband has loved pandas since he was tiny, and we finally got to see pandas in Berlin a couple of years ago. And we really enjoyed visiting our local zoo to see the tigers.

Given the title of the book, you might also find a couple of little nods to a certain film within these pages; I hope you enjoy spotting them.

But most of all I hope you enjoy the story of my heroine, Geri, who's determined to see the sunshine despite some personal tragedy, and the way she teaches Ant to see the sunshine, too.

With love,

Kate Hardy

AN ENGLISH VET IN PARIS

KATE HARDY

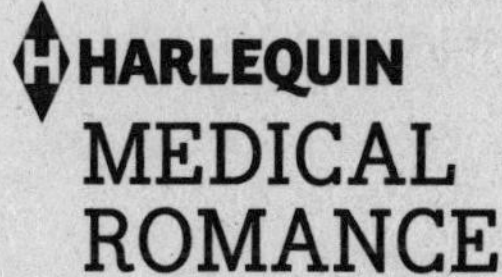

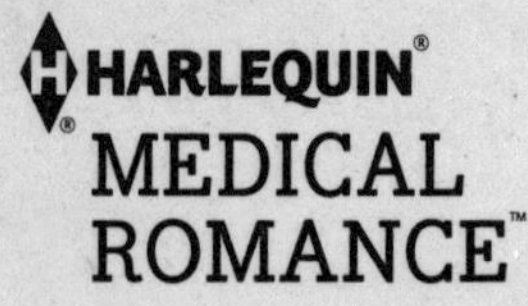

HARLEQUIN® MEDICAL ROMANCE™

Recycling programs for this product may not exist in your area.

ISBN-13: 978-1-335-73795-3

An English Vet in Paris

Harlequin Enterprises ULC
22 Adelaide St. West, 41st Floor
Toronto, Ontario M5H 4E3, Canada
www.Harlequin.com

Printed in U.S.A.

Kate Hardy has always loved books and could read before she went to school. She discovered Harlequin books when she was twelve and decided that this was what she wanted to do. When she isn't writing, Kate enjoys reading, cinema, ballroom dancing and the gym. You can contact her via her website: katehardy.com.

Books by Kate Hardy

Harlequin Medical Romance

Twin Docs' Perfect Match

Second Chance with Her Guarded GP
Baby Miracle for the ER Doc

Changing Shifts

Fling with Her Hot-Shot Consultant

Carrying the Single Dad's Baby
Heart Surgeon, Prince…Husband!
A Nurse and a Pup to Heal Him
Mistletoe Proposal on the Children's Ward
Forever Family for the Midwife
Surgeon's Second Chance in Florence
Saving Christmas for the ER Doc

Visit the Author Profile page
at Harlequin.com for more titles.

For Gerard—one day we will get to
the top of the Eiffel Tower!

**Praise for
Kate Hardy**

"Ms. Hardy has definitely penned a fascinating read in this book… Once the hero confesses to the heroine his plan for a marriage of convenience, I was absolutely hooked."

—*Harlequin Junkie* on
Heart Surgeon, Prince…Husband!

CHAPTER ONE

'ANT, I NEED your help.'

Why would the Zoo de Belvédère's head of human resources need his help? Antoine Bouvier was more used to one of the zookeepers coming in to ask him to check on an animal. Unless Marie was worrying about the health of one of her own pets, perhaps, and wanted his professional advice; but he couldn't remember her ever mentioning a cat, a dog or even a goldfish. 'What's wrong?' he asked, saving the file of the notes he was writing up.

'I brought you coffee just the way you like it.' She set the mug on his desk.

Uh-oh. This was phase one of Marie getting what she wanted: softening him up with a kindness. Ant had seen her do this with other people. Next, she'd use his name a lot: too much, in fact. Then she'd get to the subject of what she wanted and spin it to sound as if it was his idea. Finally, she'd close the deal before he could object, thank him, and swan off again before he had a chance to say a word. 'Thank you,' he said, polite yet wary. 'What did you want?'

'It's the English vet.'

The one who was starting on Monday for six months' job enrichment; their zoo in Paris was twinned with a zoo in Cambridge, and Geraldine Milligan, one of the junior vets from the English zoo, was joining his team. 'She's changed her mind and she's not coming?'

'No.' Marie looked awkward. 'The problem's with her accommodation, Ant. The windows in her apartment were meant to be replaced this week, but the builder found asbestos. The surveyor says it needs to be removed safely before anyone can live there. We're talking weeks. And finding her suitable accommodation at this late notice…' She shook her head and grimaced. 'I was wondering, Ant, could she possibly stay with you?'

'With *me*?' Ant stared at Marie, surprised.

'You have a spare room, Ant,' she pointed out.

In the townhouse in Montmartre that he'd inherited from his grandmother, two years ago; he'd been hugely grateful at the time, because it had cushioned him from some of the fallout from the wedding-that-didn't-happen.

At least he'd had somewhere to go. Somewhere to lick his wounds. A space to call his own that didn't have any memories of Céline.

'And it would be a kind gesture, Ant, as well as helping the team to bond,' she added.

All of that was true but, apart from the annoying overuse of his name, Ant had a major reservation. 'Surely it'd be awkward for her to stay with a man she's never met or had any real contact with?' The zoo's veterinary director, whose job involved negotiation and admin rather than working with animals nowadays, had arranged the secondment; Ant was simply going along with it as part of his job.

'You're both professionals, Ant,' Marie said crisply. 'I can't see why it would be a problem for her to stay with a colleague.'

'Wouldn't it be better if she stayed with one of the female members of staff?' He thought of their younger veterinary nurse. 'What about Valerie?'

Marie narrowed her eyes at him. 'Valerie lives with her parents. I can hardly impose on them, Ant.'

But she could impose on him?

As if she'd guessed what he was thinking, she said, 'It's only for a few weeks, Ant. I'm sure Dr Milligan won't be any trouble.'

Yeah, right. A woman he knew little about, other than that she was a qualified vet, had a Masters in Exotic Veterinary Medicine, and his counterpart in Cambridge was impressed enough with her skills to suggest to their director that she'd be a good addition to the team. Plus Ant had grown used to having his own space. Sharing with someone else would be strange.

'And, at this time of year, Ant, finding a hotel wouldn't be easy,' Marie continued.

Spring in Paris. The time the tourists loved most. She had a valid point.

'A few weeks,' he said. Which meant what exactly?

Before he could ask for clarification, Marie beamed at him. 'Excellent. I knew we could rely on you, Ant. Thank you very much.'

Wait, what? He hadn't agreed to anything—had he?

But he also knew that Marie was a bulldozer. It was great when you needed something done and she was working on your team; the flip side was that it was rather less great when you were on the receiving end of her pushiness.

'I wouldn't have asked you if I had another solution, Ant,' Marie said.

He didn't think that was strictly true, but

he wasn't going to waste time with an argument he knew he'd never win.

'Her train gets in to the Gare du Nord at three on Sunday afternoon.' Marie gave him the sweetest of smiles.

'I'll meet her at the station.' He didn't really have much choice. If Dr Milligan was staying with him, she'd need a key to his apartment. He could hardly tell her to wait on the doorstep or in a nearby café; besides, it wouldn't be fair to expect her to take the Métro across Paris and then find her way from the station at Montmartre to his place, particularly with a pile of luggage. 'Perhaps you could let her know the situation. And ask her for permission to give me her phone number so I can contact her to make arrangements. Give her my number, too, in case she needs to contact me about anything urgently.'

'Thank you, Ant. You're one of the good guys,' Marie said. She patted his shoulder and breezed—*hurricaned*, he thought ruefully— out of the office, her mission accomplished and leaving Ant's thoughts in complete disarray.

Sharing his space for a few weeks.

Even if Dr Geraldine Milligan turned out to be the easiest houseguest in the universe, it still meant a huge change to his life. Something that brought back memories. Something that filled him with trepidation.

The notes could wait a while. He needed to get his head round this. And the best way he knew of dealing with things that made him antsy was to go and see the tigers. Specifically Bianca, the white Bengal tiger who'd joined the Zoo de Belvédère on the same day that he had, eight years ago. As the zoo vet, Ant wasn't supposed to have favourites, but he loved the big cats, and he'd seen Bianca through three litters of cubs now; he'd been keeping a closer eye on her for the last few months, since she'd developed a liver condition. Maybe the walk over to the tigers' enclosure would help him clear his head enough to work out how he was going to deal with the situation.

The Betjeman statue at St Pancras Station was the perfect place to say goodbye to her family, Geri thought: public enough to stop her bawling her eyes out. And she really appreciated the fact that her parents and her little sister were here to wave her off.

'Geri, are you *sure* you're doing the right thing?' her father, Ben Milligan, asked. 'It's OK to change your mind if you need to. We can sort everything out.'

It reminded Geri of the speech her dad had made on her wedding day, about marrying Mark and she could change her mind. She'd said she was sure, back then. And here she was, five years later: divorced, and heartbroken…

She shook herself. Enough of the pity party. You couldn't change the past, but you could make the future better. And of course she'd made the right decision. She'd had a bit of a wobble on Friday, when the head of HR in the Zoo de Belvédère had called her to say that there was a problem with her flat and she'd be staying with Antoine Bouvier, the senior vet, instead; but then again maybe it would be good to stay in a family home rather than feeling completely alone and a bit homesick in a strange city.

Focus on the positive, she reminded herself. And the positives were always there. You only had to look for them.

'It's Paris in the spring, full of blossom and good coffee,' she said brightly. 'And it's only for six months, Dad. A secondment. A fresh start—' she forced her smile not to wobble '—and, hey, with any luck I'll be looking after a pregnant panda. Being a zoo vet doesn't get any better than knowing you're going to be one of the first to see a tiny panda cub.'

Alex, Geri's younger sister, raised her eyebrow. 'You're only taking one suitcase. Paris fashionistas will never let you get away with that.'

Geri laughed. 'I don't need to be a fashionista. Trust me, a sharp suit and Louboutins have no place when you're anaesthetising a tiger. Anyway, if I need something posh, I can always go shopping.'

Sally, Geri's mum, looked worried. 'I know we've been through this—but Paris feels so far away, love.'

'It's only a couple of hours on the train. Our girl will be fine,' Ben reassured her. He smiled at Geri. 'If you need us, just ring—any time, day or night. We'll be straight over.'

'I will,' Geri promised, mentally crossing her fingers because she knew she needed to stand on her own two feet again. Living with her parents last year while she'd done her Masters in Exotic Veterinary Medicine had meant that she'd relied way too much on them. Even this past year, after she'd moved to Cambridge, they'd fussed over her. 'Love you, Dad. Mum. Alex.' She hugged each of them in turn. 'Stop worrying. Dr Bouvier is meeting me at the station. It's all going to be fine.' Though she was aware that she was trying to convince herself as much as her family.

'Love you, Geri.' Sally held her tightly.

'Enjoy every second of Paris,' Alex said. 'Remember, your mission is to find the best crème brûlée in Paris, and then invite me over for lunch. In between the tigers, the pandas and the penguins, that is.'

'Got it.' Geri gave her parents and her sister a last hug. 'I need to go, or they'll close the gate. I'll let you know when I arrive in Paris.' Though she was pretty sure her mum would be frantically checking the location sharing app on her phone and would know the precise moment that Geri arrived at the Gare du Nord. She smiled, hoping it masked her apprehension. 'Speak to you soon.'

Had she made a huge mistake, agreeing to a six-month secondment at the zoo in Paris? Or was this the thing that would finally help her move on from the past? The way she saw it, if she was brave enough to live in a country where she hadn't spoken the language since her schooldays, then she could also be brave enough to be honest with her emotions. And that meant, the next time round, she'd pick someone who really did want the same things that she did. Someone who'd grow and change with her, rather than growing apart from her.

Besides, Paris in the spring would be

beautiful. Plus Geri had been fascinated by giant black and white pandas since she was a tiny child, and now she had the chance to work with a panda in the zoo's breeding programme—that was definitely a dream come true. Putting herself back out there, looking for the good things in life, would be a Very Good Thing. This year, on the anniversary of the day her life had fallen apart, she'd be somewhere with no sad memories; and maybe this year she'd cope better and finally start to put it behind her.

She didn't look back at her family, knowing that it would test her resolve a little too much; she scanned her ticket and her passport at the barrier, then headed for the departure lounge.

Once she was settled in her seat and the train had departed, she texted Antoine Bouvier to let him know her estimated arrival time at the Gare du Nord. Then she opened the historical thriller she'd bought for the journey, but she couldn't concentrate. Had she brought the right kind of gifts to thank her hosts? She hadn't bought flowers, not wanting them to wilt on the journey; and bringing wine to a French family would be woefully easy to get wrong. In the end, she'd settled for some really good chocolates and a tin of biscuits from Fortnum & Mason, and maybe she could take them all out for dinner one night this week.

She silently practised the phrases she'd learned that week while brushing up her language skills: *Bonjour, monsieur et madame. Merci beaucoup pour me recevoir chez vous.*

Oh, for pity's sake. She needed to ignore the apprehension causing a mass butterfly stampede in her stomach and enjoy the anticipation. This was a chance to do something she'd wanted to do for years. She was perfectly capable of negotiating life in a new city, even if her language skills were a bit rusty since her schooldays, and she'd got on well with her colleagues in Cambridge. Why would it be any different in Paris?

Stop whining and think of the positive stuff, she told herself sternly. *You're perfectly capable of doing this.*

The train journey passed swiftly, and when they came out of the other side of the Channel Tunnel there was a message on her phone from Antoine Bouvier.

Turn right when you get off the train. I'll wait for you on the west side of the station concourse.

He'd been thoughtful enough to send her a photograph of himself on Friday to help her recognise him at the station, along with a message.

Looking out for me might be a little easier than looking out for a placard with your name on it.

Geri had been surprised to see how young Dr Bouvier was. He was good-looking, in a brooding way; his dark hair had a sprinkling of grey and was cut short, his eyes were dark, and his olive skin was shadowed by a faint stubble. With a mouth that beautiful, he could've been a model for a perfume ad.

Not that she should be thinking of him in those terms. He was her new colleague—senior enough to be her boss, really—and he'd been kind enough to offer her a place to stay with his family.

She'd shaken off the stirrings of attraction and sent him a photograph in return, so he could look out for her on Sunday, too; and that had been the limit of their conversation until today.

At last, the train pulled into the Gare du Nord.

This was it.

Paris.

Her new start.

Adrenalin made her fingers tingle and she nearly dropped her suitcase. Cross with herself for the wobble—she wasn't going to let the past get in the way of her new adventure in Paris—she hauled her case off the train and turned right, scanning the crowd for a glimpse of her new colleague.

Ant surveyed the people coming from the train. He recognised Geraldine Milligan from her photograph straight away, though she was a little taller and slighter than he'd expected. Her fair hair was pulled back from her face in a scrunchie; her eyes were wide and almost navy-blue, and her mouth was a perfect Cupid's bow. She was dressed casually, in jeans, a long-sleeved T-shirt, canvas shoes and a light fleece jacket, and she looked very English.

The fact that she only had one suitcase with her surprised him. It wasn't much for a six-month stay. Or maybe she was hedging her bets and seeing how thc first few weeks went; moving to another country for six months was quite a life change.

He took a deep breath and walked towards her, holding up a hand in greeting.

She smiled when she saw him. *'Bonjour, monsieur et...'* She tailed off, before rallying with, *'Merci beaucoup pour me recevoir chez vous.'*

He hadn't expected Dr Milligan to speak in French, and he appreciated that she'd made the effort. *'De rien—'* And then he had to stop. Was she *mademoiselle* or *madame*? A quick glance told him she wasn't wearing a ring, but that didn't necessarily mean she was single. Not wanting to get it wrong, he switched to English. 'You're very welcome, Dr Milligan.'

'Call me Geri, please.' She held out her hand.

'Antoine.' He took her hand to shake it, and it felt as if he'd been galvanised. He'd never reacted to anyone like that before, even Céline, and it threw him for a moment.

'I wasn't sure how much luggage you'd have,' he said, dropping her hand and hoping that she couldn't tell how much she'd momentarily flustered him. 'Parking isn't great around here; I thought it'd be easiest to get a taxi back to my apartment,' he added. 'The queue moves fairly quickly. Shall we?' He gestured towards the taxi rank, then went to pick up her suitcase.

'Thanks, but I can manage my case myself,' she said, with the kind of smile that made it clear she wasn't being difficult.

Independent, rather, he decided. He liked that, as long as that independence was tempered with knowing to ask for help when you needed it. The welfare of the animals came before anything else, in his view. 'Of course,' he said.

In real life, Antoine Bouvier was even more attractive than his photograph, Geri thought. When he'd shaken her hand, it had sent a shiver of awareness down her spine, making her feel off balance; she really shouldn't react like that towards her new colleague, particularly if he was married. The unexpected whirl of her feelings had made her a little bit snippy about her suitcase, but hopefully he wouldn't hold the slight rudeness against her.

She followed him to the taxi rank; as he'd said, the queue moved fast, and soon he was opening the door for her to get in the back of the taxi while the driver put her case in the boot. He gave the address in rapid French, then sat next to her. Geri followed his example and looked out of the window, enjoying the views: the tall buildings with their shuttered windows and ironwork balconies, the wide cobbled streets, and the trees dappling the streets with shade. It was a far cry from the ancient narrow streets in Cambridge, dominated by the colleges and the ubiquitous cyclists.

The taxi pulled over to the kerb, and Antoine had dealt with the fare before Geri even had the chance to offer to pay. And then she was standing on the pavement, her suitcase beside her, looking up at the row of five-storey townhouses. They were built from pale stone, with wrought-iron balconies at the bottom of tall windows; there were trees along the cobbled street, and streetlights which looked like old-fashioned lanterns.

Before she could stop herself, she blurted out, 'What a beautiful building. It's so Parisian.'

Oh, way to go, Geri. How to make your new colleague think you're a babbling idiot.

'Thank you.' He shrugged. 'I guess it's easy to take it for granted. My apartment's on the top two floors. *Bienvenue à Montmartre.*'

'*Merci,*' she said with a smile.

He unlocked the door and led her through to the lobby. The lift was tiny, and the two of them only just managed to fit inside, together with her case. Geri was very, very aware of his closeness; and even more aware that the frisson down her spine was completely inappropriate. There was a huge difference between noticing the gorgeousness of a random stranger and being attracted to a new colleague who was being kind enough to let her stay with his family.

She made herself concentrate on the lift instead. It felt very French, with the glass doors looking through an ironwork grille as they rose very slowly towards the top of the building. The creaks and grinding noises sounded ominous to Geri; Antoine looked completely unbothered by them, so she decided to take her lead from him.

Not wanting to risk blurting out something inane again, she waited for him to start the conversation. Except he didn't. By the time the lift pinged to say they'd reached their floor, she was starting to feel really awkward. Maybe Antoine was the kind of dedicated vet who was brilliant with animals but not with people; hopefully his partner would put her more at ease.

He unlocked the front door, and she followed him into a hallway.

'We'll leave your case here while I give you the guided tour,' he said. 'I guess my apartment's a little upside down—the bedrooms, bathrooms and my study are on this floor, and the living quarters are on the floor above.' He gestured to the first door. 'That's my room, but feel free to choose whichever you like of the guest rooms.'

'Thank you,' she said.

'I'll show you upstairs first,' he said.

Wide stairs led up to the top floor. The walls were painted a pale biscuity colour, toning with the light wooden parquet flooring. All the ceilings had moulded cornices—the kind Geri associated with ancient European palaces—and old-fashioned wrought-iron and glass chandeliers; the tall windows meant that the rooms were full of light. The dining room was at the front of the apartment, overlooking the street, with a narrow wrought-iron balcony that ran the length of the building and held terracotta planters stuffed with red geraniums. There was a table and six chairs in the centre of the room, a traditional French sideboard that she guessed was antique and a grandfather clock that ticked loudly.

The dining room led into the living room, which was furnished with a couple of sofas, a thick Persian rug and an armoire; there were framed botanical prints on the walls, and an ornate mirror above the mantelpiece. Geri couldn't see any personal touches: no bookshelves, no photographs, or anything to suggest that this was a family home. This was strange. She was sure Marie had said Antoine Bouvier was married…or had she assumed it, because he was the senior vet at the zoo and her own boss in Cambridge was married with grown-up children?

'The fireplace is gorgeous,' she said. The old-fashioned black-leaded fireplace had a stone hearth with two wrought-iron sphinx firedogs flanking it. 'Do you have an open fire in winter?'

Antoine shook his head. 'My grandparents did, when I was small, but central heating's much less messy. Though I couldn't quite part with the fireplace during the renovations. Come and see the terrace.' He led her through to an enormous kitchen with a red-tiled floor, old-fashioned shelving and cupboards and a butler's sink but what looked like very high-tech white goods. He unlocked the back door, and she was thrilled to see a comfortable roof garden shaded with huge plants in equally huge pots, and a wrought-iron bistro table and a couple of chairs.

'It looks like the perfect place to sit and read on a summer evening.'

'With a glass of wine,' he agreed. 'Yes, it's pretty much perfect.'

'I'm really grateful to you and your partner for letting me stay,' she said. 'Finding another flat at such short notice would've been a bit daunting.'

'Yes,' he said. 'Though I should perhaps advise you now that I don't have a partner.'

She winced. 'I apologise. I thought…' Wrongly. Hideous embarrassment at her gaffe flooded through her, and she could feel the colour bursting into her cheeks. 'I'm terribly sorry.'

'Not a problem,' Ant said. 'I should've mentioned it earlier.' Though, if his fiancée hadn't fallen in love with his brother, then he would still have had a partner. Maybe they would've had a baby, by now. A little girl who'd sit on his shoulders and beam in delight when he took her to see the tigers…

But things were as they were. And he needed to put his houseguest at her ease.

He took a deep breath. 'I did suggest to Marie that you might be more comfortable sharing with someone who wasn't a single male you'd never met before, but she seemed to think we could both be professional about the situation.'

'Of course,' Geri said swiftly.

'If you prefer, I can call in a favour and stay with friends until you've found somewhere.'

'No, no—it's fine.'

Though it clearly wasn't, because she looked flustered.

'You're perfectly safe with me,' he said, wanting to reassure her that he wasn't going to make unwanted advances.

A tide of deep red swept through her face for the third time since he'd met her. She definitely wasn't the type who could hide her feelings easily, then.

Unlike Céline, who'd hidden a huge, *huge* secret until their wedding day—and then it had all come out in the most hurtful way.

Not that he was going to think about his ex. Or his brother. It was over and finished with.

'Of course I know I'm safe with you. I wouldn't have thought anything else,' Geri said. 'I'm very grateful that you're letting me stay here, even though it's all been last-minute and it must be putting you out. And it was really kind of you to meet me, though I still owe you for the taxi.'

'*De rien,*' he said, realising that he hadn't managed to stop her feeling awkward. His sister was right: he needed to brush up his social skills. 'It's fine. Really. The taxi was the least I could do. May I offer you some coffee? Wine?'

'Coffee would be lovely,' she said, looking grateful.

'I'll make it while you choose your room,' he said. Hopefully that would give them both some breathing space.

She followed him into the kitchen, where he took beans from the fridge.

'You don't need to go to that much trouble for me,' she said. 'Instant coffee's fine.'

'Instant?' He rolled his eyes. 'This is Paris.'

'There's nothing wrong with instant coffee.'

Oh, but there was. He had experience of English instant coffee, and it wasn't something he wanted to repeat. 'Let's agree to disagree,' he said. 'I'll make coffee. Go and have a look downstairs. Oh—and you need a key to the apartment.' He took the spare one from the kitchen drawer and handed it to her.

'Thank you,' she said.

He'd ground the beans and the coffee was brewed to perfection when she came back into the kitchen. 'I chose the smaller guest room,' she said. 'I hope that's all right.'

The room furthest from his. Which was a good thing—and a bad one, at the same time. He'd wanted her to choose the room because she liked it, not for any other reason. 'That's fine.'

'And I brought these from London as a small gesture of appreciation for having me.' She handed him a tin of biscuits and a box of chocolates; both bore the logo and signature colour of a very upmarket London department store. 'I thought I could take you out to dinner, to say thank you.'

'That's kind of you, but there was really no need to bring me anything. I'm sure you would've done the same for me if I'd come to Cambridge on secondment and stayed with you. Do you take milk, sugar?' He gestured to the coffee pot.

'Neither, thanks.' She accepted a cup of coffee and let him usher her onto the terrace.

'You have a beautiful apartment,' she said. 'I love the mix of ancient and modern. You said you renovated it?'

'Not all with my own hands. I hired builders to do the structural stuff,' he said.

'They did a good job. It's beautifully decorated—I loved those voile drapes at the window in my room. And the bathroom—the shape of the tiles on the floor reminds me of a honeycomb.'

'I was very nearly forced to include tiles with bees.' He rolled his eyes. 'They were my sister Amélie's choice. It's her room.'

Geri's eyes widened with obvious anxiety.

'Oh! Sorry. If you need me to move into a different room…'

'Not at all,' he said. 'She doesn't come to Paris that often, and only at certain times of the year. Fortunately for me, most of the time she's too busy making wine to come here and boss me about.' Or nag him about the family rift. He was trying to put it behind him, but he still wasn't in a place where he could forgive.

His houseguest seemed to relax again. 'I can relate to that, though actually I'm the bossy sister.'

Ant couldn't imagine Geri Milligan being bossy. If anything, she'd seemed a little lost as she'd walked through the train station. Or maybe that was because she was making such a big life change, moving to a different country for six months. He wondered what had driven her to do that. What made her tick.

'What kind of wine does your sister make?' Geri asked.

'Sancerre.' He lifted a shoulder in a half-shrug. 'It's the family business. My grandparents were winemakers, and my dad took over when they retired. When we were small, Amélie was the one who was interested in the soil and the plants; and then, as a teen, in the way the chemistry of the wine changed.

I was more interested in the vineyard's dogs and cats—and our neighbour's rescued Poitou donkey, Bertrand,' he added wryly.

'It sounds as if you were always going to be a vet.'

'Yes.' And, when he was younger, he'd thought about going into partnership with Jean-Luc: the Bouvier brothers, veterinary surgeons. Just as well he'd been drawn to zoo medicine as a student, or his career would've gone the same way as his personal life.

'I used to bandage our poor Labrador on a regular basis when I was tiny,' Geri said, 'but he always put up with it because I'd give him a biscuit as "medicine".'

Ant could imagine that. And, for a moment, he could see a small child in his mind's eye, copying her father in being a vet and 'looking after' the family pets… Except he wouldn't be the child's father. He pushed the thought away. 'Are either of your parents vets?'

'No. Dad's an accountant, Mum works in admin, and my little sister's a fitness instructor.'

'And you're really the bossy one?' He still didn't quite believe her.

She laughed. 'Alex is bossy in her classes. I couldn't move, the day after I did one of her aerobics sessions. But outside that she's a bit scatty.' She smiled. 'I'm under instructions, though, to find the best crème brûlée in Paris for when she comes to visit.' Her smile broadened. 'Which is going to be fun—both the search and her visit.'

Her laugh was lovely. Bright and sparkly. Geri was clearly close to her family, and telling him about them had taken away that lost look. Ant felt a flicker of something in his veins, something he couldn't quite pin down. A feeling so old and neglected that he barely recognised it.

He shook himself. They were talking about crème brûlée and her sister's visit—by which time Geri would be settled in her own apartment.

'Indeed.' He lifted his coffee cup in a toast. 'Welcome to Paris.'

'Thank you. I've been looking forward to this hugely.'

'It's a big change,' he said. 'What made you decide to come to Paris?'

Her face shuttered slightly. It was clearly something she wasn't comfortable talking about. He could appreciate that; he didn't like talking about bits of his life, either.

'I've always been fascinated by pandas,' she said. 'When I had the chance to work with the international breeding programme, I jumped at it.'

That was fair enough. He was thrilled to be part of it, too. And work was a safe subject. He could handle that. 'I'll introduce you to the pandas and their keeper tomorrow. I thought you could shadow me for the day, to get a feel for our routine and a chance to meet the rest of the team—and I include the keepers in our team, because they're the ones who notice when something isn't quite right with one of the animals and tell us, meaning we can treat a problem at the earliest stages.'

'That's how we work in Cambridge, too.' She looked pleased. 'I'm really glad of the chance to broaden my knowledge. And I hope I'm bringing experience with me that will be useful to others.'

'I'm sure you will,' he said. 'I'm cooking dinner for us tonight.'

'Thank you.' She paused. 'While I'm staying with you, perhaps we can take it in turns to cook—it'd be a bit of a waste of time and energy for us to cook separately, wouldn't it? And I'm very happy to do my share of the chores.'

'I have a cleaner,' Ant said. 'There's no need for a chore rota. But, yes, if you like, we can take turns in cooking.' She didn't need to know that he usually grabbed something from the staff canteen at lunchtime to eat at his desk and made himself a sandwich in the evening. His family had always been excellent hosts, and he intended to keep that tradition going. 'Are there any dietary requirements I need to know about?'

'No. I eat most things,' she said.

He suppressed the unexpected urge to tease her by suggesting frogs' legs. And that in itself was unsettling, because it was a long while since he'd been tempted to tease someone. 'I was thinking something simple. Chicken Provençal, followed by cheese and fruit?'

'That sounds lovely,' she said. 'Can I do anything to help?'

'No. Take your time to unpack and settle in,' he said. 'Dinner will be ready at seven. Would you prefer red, white or rosé wine?'

'I like all three. Whatever you feel goes best with dinner,' she said.

'*D'accord.* See you later.'

CHAPTER TWO

HER NEW COLLEAGUE was an enigma, Geri thought as she unpacked and put her things away. Antoine Bouvier had been perfectly polite to her, but she was aware that he was keeping his distance. Marie had intimated that he'd offered to let her stay with him, but his comment earlier about thinking she'd feel more comfortable staying with someone who wasn't a single male made Geri wonder whether it was more like he'd been pushed into making the offer.

She'd have to make the best of the situation. And there was a lot to be grateful for. The room was gorgeous, with voile curtains and teal drapes at the windows; the bed had a white-painted wooden frame and a duck-egg-blue patterned duvet cover. There was a white-painted wardrobe, dressing table and bedside cabinet, and a pretty blue rug was spread across the pale parquet flooring. Best of all, Geri could actually see a bit of the Sacré Coeur from the window.

Of all the places to stay in Paris, Montmartre must be one of the prettiest, she thought, and took a snap of the view to send to her family.

She glanced at her watch. There was still another hour before dinner. Antoine had made it very clear he didn't want any help in the kitchen, and she didn't want to make him feel as if he needed to entertain her. The last thing she wanted was to be an intrusive, demanding guest, even though right at that moment she felt lonely and a bit homesick and could really do with a hug. Instead, she sent cheerful messages to her family and friends along with a picture of her view, determined not to give in to the melancholy that threatened to drain her energy, then worked on her list of places she wanted to visit in Paris. If the conversation stalled over dinner, maybe her list would be something to talk about.

When she walked upstairs, the dining room table was meticulously laid with silver and crystal. She headed for the kitchen to find her host, and paused in the doorway. 'Dinner smells lovely.'

'Perfect timing,' Antoine said, not acknowledging her compliment.

'Can I take anything through?'

'The wine,' he said, taking a bottle from the fridge and uncorking it.

He brought in the food, then gestured to her to serve herself.

'This is wonderful,' she said after her first taste.

'I'm glad you like it.'

She took a sip of the wine. 'This is lovely, too. Is it one your sister made?'

'Yes.'

He didn't take the conversation further. The silence felt too awkward to bring up the topic of her Paris list, but she didn't want to eat in complete silence, either. She fell back on what she hoped would be a safe subject: work. 'You said earlier that I'd be shadowing you tomorrow. May I ask what's on the agenda?'

'I'm usually at the zoo by eight,' he said.

Just as well she was a lark rather than an owl, Geri thought.

'I'll introduce you to the team. First thing, we look at the daybook and discuss the active cases, and from there we decide what the plan is for the day. I have some things scheduled in already—we have an elephant who was stung on the eyelid yesterday, and I want to check him for swelling, plus we have an okapi with a swollen jaw who needs an X-ray.'

'Are we looking at sedation?'

'No. We've been working with conditioned behaviour,' he said. 'Okapis are quite unpredictable when they're under anaesthetic. We're doing the X-ray while she's still conscious.'

'How?'

He smiled, then, and it took Geri's breath away. When he wasn't being polite and anonymous, or silent and brooding, Antoine Bouvier was utterly gorgeous.

'She's been trained to stand still for a treat,' he said.

'That's brilliant—it reduces the stress on the okapi and takes out the risk of anaesthetic,' Geri said.

'Plus it gives the okapi some stimulation, because the keeper will do some target training first and then the okapi will stand still for the treat. Do you not do that in Cambridge?'

'We don't have okapis,' she said.

'It doesn't have to be okapis,' he pointed out. 'Any animal responds to conditioning.'

'Like Pavlov's dogs,' she said.

He smiled in acknowledgement, and her heart skipped a beat. Talking about animals was clearly a subject he liked. Wanting to keep him talking, she asked, 'Which animals are your favourites?'

'As a vet, I'm not supposed to have favourites.'

She ignored the rebuke; every vet she knew had favourites. She gave him a pointed look.

He sighed. 'All right. The tigers. We have a white Bengal tiger, Bianca. She joined the zoo the same day that I did. I'm very fond of her.'

'I look forward to meeting her,' Geri said. 'And the pandas.'

'The pandas are your favourite, I assume?'

'Absolutely. My earliest memory is seeing the pandas at London Zoo. My parents bought me a panda cuddly toy, and a book that I made them read to me every night until it fell apart.' She smiled. 'Obviously there are still pandas at Edinburgh Zoo, but not at London; since that first visit I've had to travel to get my panda fix. I got to see the babies at Berlin, the other year, and that was amazing.' She smiled at the memory. 'I'm still blown away by the fact that a cub might only weigh ninety grams at birth—around a thousand times smaller than their mum.'

'Hopefully we'll have a cub here,' he said. 'Zhen's exhibiting behaviour that means she's coming up to her fertile phase.'

The incredibly short window of two to three days in a year was one of the reasons why panda numbers were in decline. 'Perfect timing for me to join the team, then,' she said. 'Are we looking at mating her naturally with the male?'

'No. We've tried for the last two years. The year before last, Bohai—our male—was a bit clueless and didn't seem to know what to do, even when we built him a special ramp to help him. Last year, he seemed to get the idea, but Zhen wouldn't have anything to do with him,' he explained. 'This year we're going to try artificial insemination. We don't know the best timing to collect eggs from a female panda or when to transfer an embryo; AI is the only technique we can use right now.'

'I've done that with cows,' she said.

'Then you'll know about frozen sperm and thawing. Good.' He paused. 'Though it's a little different from cows, because we need to anaesthetise the bears for the procedure, and we use a catheter rather than an AI gun for insemination.'

'But it's still done slowly, I assume.'

He nodded.

'You said you anaesthetise both bears?'

'Yes. We'll take fresh sperm from Bohai

under anaesthetic, mix it with thawed frozen sperm from the international cryopreservation bank, and then inseminate Zhen under anaesthetic. Four students are coming in from the university to observe, though I think it'll be useful for them to have a bit of hands-on practice.' He raised an eyebrow. 'I assume you're experienced with anaesthetics?'

'I worked with large animals at my practice, before I did my Masters and switched to zoo medicine,' she said. 'Although obviously I haven't worked with a panda before, a lot of the principles are the same.'

'Very true,' he acknowledged. 'What made you switch to zoo medicine?'

Because working with farm animals had led to an event that had changed her life utterly—and broken her heart. Not that she was going to dump that on a stranger. 'I'd always been interested in exotics,' she said. 'After my divorce, I took a long look at my life and what needed to change.'

And making a big career change had helped to distract her from the misery of the miscarriage, the shock of realising that she and Mark wanted very different things, and the hard to face knowledge that having the family of her dreams might be a lot more difficult now. Not that Antoine Bouvier needed to know that; she didn't want his pity. She wanted him to see her for the competent professional she was. 'Can I ask why you're using a mix of fresh and frozen sperm?' she asked.

'Bohai might not produce enough fresh sperm; the frozen acts as a safety net. The mixture helps with genetic diversity and increases the chance of pregnancy, because the sperm cells in the frozen semen are already activated,' he explained.

'And then we wait,' she said. 'If it works, Zhen will have the cub somewhere in the next fifty to one hundred and sixty days, depending on when the egg implants. It still amazes me that pandas have embryonic diapause.' The fertilised egg started to divide, and then the process stopped; the embryo might not attach to the panda's uterine wall until weeks later, and only then would the embryo's development continue.

'Not only pandas,' he reminded her. 'Kangaroos, mustelids and other species of bears do the same thing.'

'Which is very likely to do with waiting until it's the optimum time for the embryo's survival,' she said. 'Though it makes it hard for us to know what's happening.'

'Especially because pandas often have

pseudopregnancies, where they exhibit the same behaviour and similar hormonal changes as if they're actually pregnant,' he said. 'This is going to be an interesting project for you.'

'And I'm a sucker for babies,' she said. 'There's nothing like a cuddle from a kitten or a puppy.'

'Do you have pets back in England?' he asked.

'No,' she said. 'With the hours I worked—' not to mention that Mark had liked their home to be absolutely pristine, which in hindsight should've been a warning sign '—I didn't have the time a pet deserved.' She'd made a fuss of her patients instead: from the cattle to the farm dogs and cats, and the pigs to the sheep.

The sheep that unwittingly had been her downfall.

'As I can't see any evidence of a dog, do I assume you have a sleek Parisian cat who's prowling the rooftops somewhere?' she asked, trying to push the memories away.

'No. Like you, I work long hours; I don't think it's fair to have a dog or cat.' He shrugged. 'But I enjoy my job—and my patients.'

But even work turned out to be a subject that died out by the time they got to the cheese and fruit course, and when she asked him about his tastes in music, cinema and books she felt as if she were prying rather than trying to get to know a new colleague and housemate.

'What time do we need to leave tomorrow?' she asked.

'It's a ten-minute walk to Pigalle station, then about twenty minutes on the Métro to the zoo. We don't have to change lines,' he said. 'I'm sorry, I should've bought bacon and eggs for your breakfast.'

'Actually, I usually have cereal—though toast is fine by me,' she said. 'Or whatever you usually have for breakfast.' She didn't want to be a difficult guest.

'Coffee and a baguette with conserves,' he said.

'That sounds lovely,' she said. 'As you cooked dinner, I'll wash up.' Before he could voice the protest she could see in his expression, she reminded him, 'We agreed to share the chores.'

'I don't leave the dishes for my cleaner,' he said, 'but I do have a dishwasher.'

And she'd bet he was fussy about how it was stacked.

As if her thoughts had shown on her face, he said, 'It will take me two minutes to stack it.'

Though he did at least let her help bring the crockery through. 'If you'll excuse me, I have some paperwork to catch up on,' he said. 'Feel free to use the television, though I'm afraid I don't watch it much and I'm not sure what kind of English programmes you can access.'

'I think I can access my streaming account abroad, but that's probably easiest on my laptop,' she said.

'*D'accord.* Sorry, I should have given you the Wi-Fi password earlier,' he said. 'Let me get that for you.' He grabbed his phone, and a couple of seconds later her phone pinged with a message that was clearly his Wi-Fi code.

'Is it all right to make myself a cup of tea?' she asked. 'I assumed you drink coffee rather than tea in France. I brought some Earl Grey teabags with me.'

'Please, make yourself at home,' he said. 'I do have some tisanes—chamomile and peppermint—but I'm afraid I didn't think to buy English tea.'

'I don't expect you to buy things especially for me,' she said. 'And I'd prefer to go halves on the shopping while I'm staying with you.

I'm cooking tomorrow night, though I could do with some pointers about where to shop.'

He dipped his head in acknowledgement. 'There's a row of shops in the next street—the baker, the butcher, the greengrocer and the *fromagerie*—and the supermarket's ten minutes away. I'll send you the addresses. Then you can find them on your phone's map.'

'Thank you. Is there anything you don't eat?' she asked.

He shrugged. 'I'm not fussy.'

'All right. I'll see you tomorrow at breakfast then, I guess,' she said.

Unsettling. That was what Geraldine Milligan was.

Ant wasn't sure what it was about her that disconcerted him. The keenness of her blue eyes—especially as he had a nasty feeling that she could see right through him. The brightness of her smile. The way she hadn't let him retreat into silence but had persuaded him to chat to her; he was more used to being left alone to brood under his dark cloud.

And all that meant she had the ability to turn his quiet, ordered life upside down. He'd need to be very, very careful. He couldn't face that kind of disorder and unhappiness again.

* * *

The next morning, Antoine had already made a pot of coffee before Geri came upstairs. She joined him in a breakfast of toasted baguette and a sharp yet incredibly fruity orange marmalade; then they took the Métro to the Zoo de Belvédère. The train was too noisy and crowded for them to talk on the journey; he seemed to switch into tour guide mode when they reached the park, and he pointed out various bits of interest for her.

At the zoo, he introduced her to the rest of the veterinary team and senior keepers; then they checked the daybook, and the jobs were shared out.

'We'll start with the okapi,' Antoine said, and took her over to the enclosure along with the portable X-ray machine. 'Geri, this is Sylvie, who looks after the okapi. Sylvie, this is Geri from the Cambridge zoo, who's working with us for the next six months. We'd like to X-ray Nia.'

'Then we can get to the bottom of that sore jaw. Exccllent.' Sylvie smiled warmly. 'We'll do a little bit of target training with her, first, and then she'll stay still for the X-ray.'

'She's beautiful,' Geri said as they went over to the training enclosure. 'With those stripes, you'd think okapis were related to zebras rather than giraffes.'

Sylvie nodded. 'Especially as only the males have the ossicones. It still amazes me that we've only known about their existence for a little over a century.'

'Are you OK to operate the X-ray?' Antoine asked Geri.

'Of course,' Geri said.

She was fascinated by the way Sylvie used a piece of wood as a target; Nia touched it with her nose and got a treat of acacia leaves as a reward. Sylvie repeated it a couple of times.

'Is acacia their favourite food?' Geri asked.

'And some fruits.' Sylvie grinned. 'Hey, you know what a giraffe's favourite fruit is? A neck-tarine.'

Geri laughed. 'Love it. I'll remember that one.'

But Antoine, she noticed, barely cracked a smile at Sylvie's joke.

Did he hate bad puns? Or was he simply reserved with everyone at work? Geri couldn't quite work out what made him tick.

Finally, Sylvie finished the training and Nia stayed still while Geri sorted out the X-ray, and then Sylvie gave the okapi more treats.

'We have a dentist in the next *arrondisse-ment* who specialises in animal teeth,' Antoine told Geri. 'We'll send the X-rays over to her for assessment, and then we'll know what's happening with Nia's jaw and what we need to do next to make her comfortable again.' He gave Sylvie a brief nod. 'I'll come and see you as soon as we hear something. Thanks for your help.'

They paid a couple more visits to animals who needed checking—the elephant who'd been stung on his eyelid, where Antoine was happy that the swelling was going down and no extra treatment was needed, and a tortoise with a broken toenail, where thankfully it wasn't infected and she'd be fine.

'And now for the bit you've been looking forward to,' he said, taking her to the panda enclosure. 'This is Pierre, who looks after our pandas.'

'Zhen's our female,' Pierre said. 'Her name means "precious". And Bohai's the male; his name means "sea".'

'Good names,' Geri said. She got as close to the glass as she could. 'And oh, they're *gorgeous*.'

'How are they doing?' Antoine asked.

'Zhen's a bit restless,' Pierre said. 'She's wandering in the enclosure, walking backwards with her tail up and playing in the water.'

These were all signs that the panda was heading towards ovulation, Geri knew.

'She's vocalising more,' Pierre said, and as if on cue Zhen started to bleat and chirp.

'Bohai's vocalising, too, and keeping her in his sight,' Pierre added. 'I'm waiting to grab today's urine samp—' He broke off as Zhen started to urinate. 'I'll be back in a minute,' he said.

'She's definitely getting closer,' Antoine said. 'Hopefully Pierre can manage to get that urine sample before it all soaks into the earth, and we'll check the lab results against yesterday's sample.'

'I'm really excited about this,' she said. 'Getting to know the pandas and being involved in the breeding programme.'

'It's a privilege,' Antoine agreed.

Pierre managed to get the sample. 'For the last week, I've kept a sealed bag with a sterile syringe in my pocket,' he said wryly.

'Just as well,' Antoine said, and put the labelled phial into his bag before taking Geri around a couple more enclosures.

At lunchtime, Antoine grabbed a sandwich along with the others in the staff canteen, but left early, saying that he needed to catch up with paperwork. 'Stay and take your full break,' he directed Geri.

'Don't take it personally,' Valerie, the junior veterinary nurse, said. 'It's amazing that he stayed with us for as long as he did. He normally eats at his desk.'

'He's a bit remote with everyone, then, not only m—?' Geri stopped and grimaced. 'I'm sorry. I didn't mean to be rude and judgemental.'

'Of course you didn't. Antoine's fabulous with the animals, patient and kind,' Valerie said. 'But it's fair to say he's not really a people person.'

'He used to be,' Émilie, the senior veterinary nurse, said. 'Before—' She wrinkled her nose. 'No, it's not fair to gossip.'

'I won't say anything,' Geri promised. 'But if there's something I ought to know so I don't…' She stopped, her vocabulary deserting her, and circled her hand to show she was searching for the right phrase.

'Faire une gaffe?' Valerie supplied.

Émilie nodded. 'Let's say his ex broke his heart, a couple of years ago, and he doesn't let anyone close now. Except maybe his parents and his sister, and they live in the Loire.' She gave a very Gallic shrug.

Geri knew how that felt. Been there, done

that—but her family and friends hadn't let her withdraw, and she'd tried hard to find the sunshine ever since. 'That's a shame,' she said quietly. 'I'll be tactful. Thank you for warning me.'

The conversation turned to Paris and advice from everyone about the best times to visit the more popular tourist spots, as well as suggestions for places she might enjoy exploring. At the end of her lunch break, she headed back to Antoine's office.

'What's the agenda for this afternoon?' she asked.

'More rounds,' he said. 'Though I need to make a couple of phone calls, first. The urine sample's exactly what I hoped it would be— her oestrogen levels have peaked. It looks as if she's ovulating. Tomorrow morning, we're doing the AI.'

'That's fantastic news,' she said.

'I'll do the initial sedation,' he said, 'and then we'll have the usual team of three on anaesthesia—one on airway management, one monitoring the anaesthetic drugs, and one doing the record-keeping—while I do the insemination procedure. That means you, Jacques and Émilie.'

'Which do you want me to do?' she asked.

'Your choice,' he said.

'Airway management,' she decided.

'That's fine.'

In between the rounds, Geri met Marie, the head of HR, who seemed warm and effusive.

At the end of the day, the veterinary nurses left—as did Jacques, the other vet.

'What time do you normally leave the zoo?' she asked Antoine.

He spread his hands and shrugged. 'It depends on the paperwork. Unfortunately, today is a big paperwork day. Will you be all right getting back to the apartment on your own?'

Geri wondered if he was using the paperwork as an excuse to avoid her company, but smiled sweetly. 'Of course. What time would you like dinner?'

His eyes widened slightly. 'I, uh…'

'Seven?' she suggested.

'You really don't have to cook for me.'

'I can take you out to dinner, if you'd prefer,' she said.

That was definite panic in his eyes, then, and she remembered what Émilie had said. This wasn't about her; Antoine was clearly still hurting from whatever had happened with his ex. She knew how that felt. Mark had moved on, and she was glad he was happy; at the same time, she wished things could've been different. That they'd wanted the same things. That her fertility wasn't in question, post-Q fever. 'I'll make something flexible,' she said. 'Text me when you're twenty minutes away, and it'll be ready five minutes after you get in.'

'*D'accord,*' he said.

Geri navigated the Métro and, with the help of her phone and the maps, found the shops Antoine had recommended. He was probably expecting her to cook something stodgy and English; she planned to surprise him.

Ant found it hard to concentrate on his paperwork; he knew it was because of Geri. She just *unsettled* him.

Eventually he closed down his computer, headed for the Métro, and texted Geri to let her know when he was twenty minutes away.

He could smell something delicious as soon as he walked into the apartment. For an odd moment, he felt as if he should've brought flowers. But this was his apartment and Geri was his houseguest; bringing flowers for her would've been inappropriate and made them both feel embarrassed.

When he walked upstairs, she appeared in the kitchen doorway and smiled. His heartbeat went up a couple of notches, and he had to breathe deeply to bring it down again. This was ridiculous. A smile shouldn't make him feel like this. He'd been perfectly fine on his own, these last couple of years. He wasn't looking to change his situation. At all. And definitely not with someone who was only here temporarily.

'Hi. Is your paperwork all wrestled into submission?' she asked.

'Something like that,' he said. 'Dinner smells good.'

She went pink and looked pleased. 'I hope you like it. You did say you ate anything.' She gave him a wicked smile. 'Though I did think about cooking roast beef and Yorkshire pudding.'

'*Les rosbifs.*' The phrase slipped out before he could stop it.

She laughed. 'Yeah. That's how I thought you'd react. One of my best friends at uni taught me her mum's recipe for Keralan chicken curry. I made flatbreads to go with it, but I'm also cooking rice and dhal. And I thought we could eat on the terrace, as it's a nice evening.'

'Can I do anything to help?'

'Sit down. It'll be ready in five minutes. Oh, you could take the jug of lassi out of the fridge, if you like.'

She'd even made a traditional Indian drink? 'That's impressive.'

She smiled. 'It's really not that difficult.'

Geri's smile definitely had the power to scramble his brain. Ant knew he'd need to be careful. Especially because, when he went out into the roof garden, it felt incredibly intimate. She'd laid the bistro table with simple bowls and his everyday cutlery rather than the family silver, and it felt like the perfect cosy evening for two. It was something he hadn't done since Céline, and it made him feel awkward.

But then he stopped having time to feel strange about it, because she brought out the dishes of food and loaded the table.

The curry was excellent; the spices were beautifully balanced. 'I don't often eat Indian food,' he said. 'This is really good.'

'You're welcome. I know I made way too much, except for the rice, but it's freezable— or maybe we can have leftovers tomorrow night.'

'Leftovers sounds good to me,' he said. 'Did you enjoy your first day at the zoo?'

She nodded. 'And I'm really looking forward to tomorrow.'

'We'll be doing the annual health check for the pandas as well as the AI procedure,' he said. 'Weight, height, teeth and bloods, for starters.'

'That makes sense,' she said.

They chatted about the pandas—a welcome safe subject—until they'd finished eating and cleared away. Ant made a pot of coffee, and they returned to the roof garden.

'I was checking the roster today,' she said, 'and it says I have Wednesday off.'

'Do you have any plans?' he asked.

'I'd like to start ticking things off my Paris list,' she said. 'The roster said you're off on Wednesday, too. I was wondering…' She looked at him shyly. 'Would you like to come with me?'

He really hadn't expected that, and it knocked him off balance.

Part of him wanted to go with her; but part of him didn't want to let her get any closer. He had a feeling that Geri Milligan could be seriously dangerous to his peace of mind. 'It's kind of you to ask,' he said, 'but, actually, I was planning to go in to work on Wednesday—I want to check on the pandas myself, as it'll be the day after the AI.'

She smiled brightly at him. 'No problem. Just a thought.'

But he'd seen the momentary sag of disappointment in her shoulders, and he knew he'd caused it. Guilt flickered through him. Would it be that difficult to show her round the city? He could even dress it up as work: helping his new colleague settle in and make her feel part of the team. It would be the kind thing to do.

Though it would also mean letting her past his barriers, and he wasn't ready to let anyone in. And he could do with a tiny bit of distance between them right now, too. Before he let her tempt him. 'You cooked,' he said. 'I'll clear up.'

Her expression showed that she knew it was an excuse to avoid her, and guilt washed through him again. It wasn't her fault. But explaining to her was too complicated. 'I'll see you later,' he muttered, and headed for the kitchen.

CHAPTER THREE

TUESDAY MORNING WAS full on. Antoine had started an hour and a half earlier than usual to give himself time to check on any animals that needed urgent help, and then checked the operating theatre so everything his team needed was in place. Just before the operation was due to start, he made sure everyone knew what their role was: Geri on airway management, Jacques on anaesthesia and Émilie on record-keeping.

'I'm trying to keep the number of people around minimal while the pandas are awake; then they won't feel crowded and it's less stressful for them. The zoo directors and the visiting lecturer can observe the actual operations while the pandas are under anaesthetic, and the four students can help with the procedures under our direction. Does that work for everyone?' he asked.

The team all murmured their assent.

He was efficient, without being abrupt, Geri thought, and it was clear that the animals were his top priority. She liked the fact that he put them before any office politics—and she really appreciated that he noticed the moments where she was struggling to keep up and quietly translated from French to English for her, without making a big deal of it.

'Good. Any questions or issues?' He paused for a moment. 'OK. I'll bring the students in now.' He disappeared and returned with four final-year veterinary students, then introduced them to his team.

'Pierre, I know we've had the keeper team monitoring the pandas overnight, but can you confirm that Zhen and Bohai haven't eaten or drunk anything for the last twelve hours?' Antoine asked.

'They haven't eaten or drunk anything,' the keeper said, 'and they're both a bit grumpy about missing their breakfast. We'll supplement the bamboo this afternoon, once they're round from the anaesthetic.'

'Good.' Antoine looked at the students. 'I'm sure you all know this, but why am I asking about food and drink?'

'To avoid any risk of regurgitation or pulmonary aspiration of the stomach contents during anaesthesia,' one of the students said.

'Exactly.' Antoine gave one of his rare smiles, and Geri was unsettled by the sudden flash of heat down her spine. This was *work*, she reminded herself. She needed to focus on her job.

'Some of the team are giving the enclosure a thorough clean while the procedures are being done,' Pierre said. 'We'll be draining the pools, disinfecting the floors and the rock features, then refilling the pools and the feeders.'

Antoine nodded. 'Let's get going. I prefer to use a hand syringe for the anaesthesia, where I can, rather than a dart. We'll start with getting Bohai—our male,' he explained to the students, 'in the restraint cage.'

Ant glanced at Geri, hoping she'd pick up the cue to ask a question. 'Why do we use the restraint cage?' she asked.

'It keeps them safe—so they won't fall or hurt themselves during a procedure,' one of the students said.

She smiled. 'That's one reason. And another?' When none of them answered, she said, 'I have a very soft spot for pandas, but are they as cute and cuddly as most people think?'

Good question, Ant thought. She was making them consider the reasons behind the clinical decisions. And he liked the fact that she was practical, even though the pandas were her favourite.

'No. They're bears,' a student said. 'They're dangerous.'

'Just like a black bear or a polar bear, though pandas aren't quite as heavy,' Geri agreed. 'Using the cage means we're out of reach of their claws and their teeth.'

'Absolutely,' Ant said. 'We need to be safe, too, or we can't treat our patients properly.'

They left the examination room for the panda enclosure, with the four students in tow. Pierre encouraged Bohai into the cage; then Ant knelt by the cage with the bear's back towards him and gently scratched the panda's back. Bohai grunted with pleasure, and Ant kept talking to him calmly while he administered the injection. He continued soothing the bear and giving a running commentary to the students while they waited for the sedative drug to take effect; a couple of minutes later, Bohai's head started drooping, and within a quarter of an hour it was safe for them to open the cage. Ant checked the panda's level of consciousness and vital signs, took a phial of blood, then covered the bear's eyes with a blindfold. 'I know he's under anaesthetic, but this helps to minimise external stimuli,' he explained to the students.

Geri put a face mask on the bear. 'Why do we need this?' she asked. When none of the students answered, she said, 'We need to keep his oxygen saturation levels up during transport. Where's the best place to put the pulse clip?'

'His tongue or his cheek,' one of the students said.

'Why not an ear?' she asked.

Again, Ant liked the way she challenged the students. He rather thought that she could challenge *him*, if he gave her the chance. She'd push him out of his comfort zone and make him engage with the world again; and he wasn't sure if the idea intrigued or terrified him more.

'Because the reading won't be good enough, and it's also too easy for the clip to slip off,' one of the others said.

'Perfect.' She smiled at the first student who'd answered. 'Put the clip on his tongue, and then I'll check it.'

Once the clip was in place, between them they gently put Bohai onto a tarpaulin, checked his weight and height, then transported him to the main examination room.

'I'm putting a cuff round his forelimb to track his blood pressure,' Geri said.

As they expected, Bohai's blood pressure had risen initially, but finally Geri was happy that the bear was relaxed and ready for intubation. With the help of two of the students, she prepared his jaw to check his upper airway. 'Dental check, first,' she said, and let the students all check the bear's teeth.

'It all looks fine to me,' the last one said.

Geri checked, too. 'No problems—no chips or cracks, or anything that makes me think we need to X-ray him,' she said. 'Now, we'll spray lidocaine on his vocal cords, to reduce the risk of his larynx going into spasm as we intubate him,' she explained. She inserted the tube, inflated the cuff and used a stethoscope to check his breath sounds, before getting the students to listen and check it too.

'Bilateral breath sounds OK,' the last one confirmed to Antoine.

Antoine gave Geri a nod of approval that made her feel warm all over. They might be a bit awkward with each other outside work, but they were definitely on the same page when they were at the zoo.

Once the airway was secured and IV access was ready, Jacques gave the bear a balanced electrolyte solution to help keep his fluids up. Finally, Antoine did the electroejaculation procedure to collect the sperm from Bohai, explaining to his audience what he was doing and why, and then Jacques administered an antiemetic.

'Are we ready to wake him?' Antoine asked.

'Ready,' Jacques and Geri confirmed.

Between them, they moved Bohai to the recovery cage; as soon as his swallowing reflex returned, Geri deflated the endotracheal tube and withdrew it carefully. They monitored him until he lifted his head, and finally got to his feet again. Once Antoine was satisfied that the bear was safe to be back in his enclosure, they took him back; one of Pierre's team stayed to feed Bohai his usual breakfast of bamboo.

They went through the same process to anaesthetise Zhen, ready for the insemination, and do her health checks.

'We're using a mix of fresh semen from Bohai and thawed frozen sperm from the international cryopreservation bank,' Antoine told the students. 'A panda has a small uterus; we need to empty Zhen's bladder first with a catheter, then insert the semen via an inseminating catheter.'

Once the procedure was done, they reversed the anaesthesia, kept a check on Zhen as she recovered, then finally took her back into her enclosure.

During the debrief, Antoine patiently answered every question from the students, and made sure that Geri, Jacques, Émilie and Pierre also had the chance to answer questions. This was a different side of Antoine, Geri thought; given that he'd seemed a bit distant with his colleagues yesterday, she'd expected him to have little patience with the students. Today he appeared more relatable—and much more likeable. She noticed that the female student kept giving him covert glances; in her shoes, Geri rather thought she would've been doing the same. Not only because Antoine was good-looking, but because he was clearly passionate about his work, and that passion was captivating.

What would it be like if Antoine showed that same passion outside his work? She couldn't help wondering, and again it sent a wave of heat through her.

Once their visitors had left, they carried on with the rest of their normal day's routine, though she noticed that Antoine skipped lunch and the afternoon break to check on the pandas.

He was reluctant to leave, only agreeing

when Pierre promised to call him at home if his team was in the slightest bit worried about the pandas.

It was too noisy on the Métro to talk, but once they were back at Antoine's flat Geri looked at him. 'Sit down. I'll make some fresh flatbread and rice, and heat up yesterday's leftovers. We were in early, and you didn't even stop for lunch.'

'I wanted to keep an eye on the pandas,' he said. 'Anaesthesia's always a worry.'

'Is this the first time we've performed panda AI at our zoo?'

He nodded. 'The pandas have been at the zoo for four years now. The first year, we missed Zhen's fertile window; the next two years, as I told you earlier, mating naturally didn't work. This year, we wanted to give her the best chance of having a cub.'

'Let's hope we're lucky this time,' she said. 'I guess we'll know at some point in the next six months.'

'If the embryo implants, and provided Zhen doesn't have a pseudopregnancy,' he said. 'We'll have to persuade her into having an ultrasound in three months' time. According to Pierre, she'll do a lot for honey water or sweet potato.'

'More Pavlov stuff,' she said lightly.

'And enrichment,' he said. 'The panda team put the bears' favourite fruit and veg in puzzle cubes and hide them around the enclosure. As well as having to hunt for the cubes, the pandas have to figure out the right angles to hold them to get the treats.'

'It's a million miles from how zoos were when I was a child,' Geri said.

'And me,' he said. 'I always thought I'd work with farm animals—after Bertrand the Poitou—but I had the chance to do a final-year project here when I was a student, and that was it for me.'

It was similar to her own career progression, but Geri didn't want to talk about the farm animals she'd loved working with and the way her life had subsequently imploded. She changed the subject. 'You were good with the students.'

'I enjoy teaching. Especially when the students' questions challenge me to further my own knowledge.' He shrugged. 'But I prefer practice. You were good with the students, too. Very clear in your explanations.'

'I like working with people as well as animals,' she said. 'But I'm enjoying the challenge of zoo medicine—using what I know and applying it to different animals.'

'Indeed.'

She could tell he'd gone remote on her again, but she wasn't going to take it personally. 'I'll go and sort dinner,' she said.

The next morning, Ant left early. He felt a bit guilty about abandoning Geri on her first day off, but reminded himself that she wasn't his responsibility; she was an adult, and she was perfectly capable of sightseeing in Paris on her own. But all the same he nipped over to the boulangerie in the neighbouring street before he went to the zoo, to buy her a couple of croissants, and left her a little note next to the bag in the kitchen.

Thought you might like these for breakfast. Enjoy sightseeing. I'll sort dinner tonight. A

By the time he arrived at the zoo, she'd texted him.

Merci beaucoup pour les croissants. À bientôt.

He liked the fact she was trying to do as much as she could in French rather than relying on her own language all the time. And the unexpected friendship growing between them made him feel warm inside.

To his relief, Zhen and Bohai had no after-effects from the anaesthetic, and he spent a busy day doing rounds and checking on a penguin with a possible case of bumblefoot. He was scanning recipes and deciding what to cook for dinner when his phone buzzed.

He glanced at the screen and frowned. His sister didn't normally call him at this time of day. 'Is everything all right, Mélie?'

'Yes, fine,' she said. 'Well, mostly.'

'What's wrong?'

'I, um… I know one of us should've told you earlier.'

Dread knifed through him. 'What's happened? Is Maman or Papa ill?'

'No, nothing like that.' She dragged in a breath. 'It's not bad news. But it's going to hurt you, and… I'm sorry for that. You know I wouldn't hurt you for the world. You're my brother and I love you.'

'I know,' he said. 'Mélie, just tell me.'

'Jean-Luc. He and Céline…um…had a little girl this morning.'

The little girl that should've been his.

And nobody in his family had breathed a word to him throughout the whole of Céline's pregnancy. They'd shut him out. For a second, Ant couldn't breathe. It felt as if he was in some kind of vacuum; the only thing that existed was stinging hurt.

But he didn't want his sister or his parents worrying about him. He pulled himself together. 'I see,' he said.

'Ant, I know one of us should've told you before.'

Yes, they should've done. But he knew why they hadn't. 'You all still tread on eggshells around me,' he said. 'I take it you were the one who drew the short straw.'

'Ant, you know we all love you. And we miss you.' She sighed. 'I *knew* I should've come to see you about this instead of phoning you.'

'We're both busy at work. Why waste a day travelling? You were right to phone me instead.'

'I'm still sorry. I know how much you loved Céline. And I wish things were different.'

'Things are as they are,' Ant said. 'You can't help who you fall in love with.'

'Just why did she have to fall in love with our brother?'

Yeah. He'd asked himself that, so many times. The whole thing was a mess. The gap they'd left in his life was still there, and he still didn't know how to deal with that.

'Are you OK?' Amélie asked.

'Yes.' Because he was going to stuff all the feelings down in a little box in a corner of his heart, and lock them up tightly before they could do any more damage. 'Mélie, I love you, but I need to cook dinner. Geri will be back soon.'

'Geri?'

'The English vet. I told you about her last week,' Ant reminded her. 'She's staying with me—in your room, actually—because the builders found asbestos in her flat, and I have room here. Marie thought it would be a good idea if she stayed with me until the zoo can find her another place.'

'Is she nice?'

'She's good with the animals. I think the secondment will go well.'

Amélie sighed. 'That isn't what I asked.'

He knew that, but it was all she was going to get. 'I'll speak to you soon,' he said. 'Give Maman and Papa my love.'

'Why don't you come and tell them your-self?'

'Because I'm really busy at the zoo.' And because his parents would naturally want to see lots of their firstborn grandchild, and Ant didn't want to risk bumping into his brother or his ex. Not until he'd had a chance to process this news and work out how he felt.

But, despite telling his sister that he was absolutely fine, he was very much out of sorts. To the point where he burned dinner. Twice. Deciding to give up and order a pizza or something when Geri came back from her sightseeing, Ant scrubbed the kitchen. Which didn't help, because cleaning didn't occupy his head anywhere near enough. He had no paperwork from the zoo to do—at least, nothing he could access from home—and he'd never really been one for watching the television.

Nothing would push the pictures out of his head.

Céline, holding a baby, her face glowing with love...

By the time he heard the front door close behind Geri, he was in a thoroughly foul mood. One which got even worse because she was bubbling over about her day as a tourist in Paris.

'The Louvre is amazing!' she said. 'I admit the *Mona Lisa* was a little bit disappointing, because I didn't expect it to be that small. But I saw tons of beautiful paintings. And the Tuileries were full of blossom—like pink fluffy clouds, and the scent was incredible. It didn't matter that it poured with rain while I was in the queue because then there was an enormous rainbow, and more rainbows inside by the upside-down pyramid, and—'

'You really are *un petit rayon du soleil*, aren't you?' he cut in.

As soon as the words came out of his mouth, he knew how horrible he was being. How unfair. None of this was her fault and she didn't deserve him venting his spleen on her. But he couldn't stop himself.

Her eyes narrowed as she translated it mentally. 'Says the man who's determined to be the rain—and spill the gloom over everyone else's parade.'

He knew he probably deserved that, but it still rankled.

'What's your problem, Antoine?' she asked.

'Nothing.' He turned away.

'Oh, no. You're not getting away with that,' she said. 'Snapping at me and then pretending there's nothing wrong—when you've been scrupulously polite and kind with me. A bit distant at times, yes, but always polite. And you were sweet enough to buy me croissants for breakfast this morning. Has something happened with the pandas?'

'No. Everything's fine at the zoo.'

'I'm glad to hear it—but everything's clearly

not fine with you,' she said. She sniffed, then frowned. 'Bleach and burned toast.'

It was obvious. He might as well admit it. 'Burned chicken, actually.'

She raised an eyebrow. 'I can't believe that someone as meticulous as you would forget that you were cooking something.'

She was too perceptive for his own good. 'I just had some news that…' He waved a hand in a circle, hoping it would be enough to explain.

'Upset you enough to burn dinner and snap at me?'

He winced. 'I apologise. I shouldn't have taken out my temper on you.'

'No, you shouldn't—but, even though I don't know you very well, this feels out of character.' She looked concerned. 'Can I do anything to help?'

'No.'

'No, because it's not something fixable, or no, because you're out of sorts and want to brood about it on your own?'

Razor-sharp perceptive, he amended mentally. 'Both, I guess.'

'Don't move,' she said. 'I'll be back in a couple of minutes.'

He heard the kettle boiling and some banging around; he could definitely smell vanilla—or was it chocolate?—and then the microwave pinged.

What was his houseguest up to?

A few moments later, she came back into the living room with a tray.

'The English answer to everything,' she said. 'Tea and cake.'

'That's *tea*?' He looked at the cup with its extremely pale beige contents. It looked like no tea he'd ever been served before. And what exactly was in the mug with a teaspoon balanced on top?

'It's Earl Grey, and probably not how a fastidious Frenchman would drink it,' she said. 'Actually, I'd get flayed in England for making tea like this, too, but I like mine weak and milky. And the cake's a chocolate mug cake. Best thing ever when you need a quick carb fix.'

It looked appalling, and it really wasn't the sort of thing he'd eat; but it was an incredibly kind gesture, and right at that moment Ant didn't know whether to laugh or cry. 'Thank you,' he said. 'I don't deserve this.'

'You're a bit of a panda,' she said. 'Not very sociable. But you've clearly had a rubbish day, and I wouldn't be a very good houseguest if I left you to stew.'

She thought he was like a panda? A solitary beast who didn't socialise?

Then again, she had a point. Since the day of the-wedding-that-wasn't, he'd kept everyone at a distance. Including his family. He hadn't been able to bear seeing the pity in their eyes, even when they tried to hide it—and he hated that his family was split. Yes, his brother was technically in the wrong; but, as he'd told his sister, you couldn't help who you fell in love with. Jean-Luc had tried to resist his feelings. So had Céline. But it had been too much for them.

Ant didn't even know where to begin knitting his family back together again.

'I apologise,' he said.

'Eat your cake while I make one for me, drink your tea, and then talk,' she said. 'I know you don't know me very well, either, but I assure you I'm not a gossip. I won't repeat anything you say to me. When things are going wrong, sometimes talking about it can take the pressure out of your head.'

He didn't have an answer to that.

The tea was vile, and the cake a bit sweet for his taste, but he appreciated the kindness behind it. And the fact that she'd left the room for a couple of minutes to give him a breathing space.

'Thank you,' he said when she returned with a second mug cake and cup of milky tea.

'De rien.' She gave a half-shrug.

He couldn't help smiling. 'It looks as if we're making a Parisienne out of you already.'

She wrinkled her nose, and he thought how cute she looked.

'A Parisienne would no doubt serve this tea with lemon, not a ton of milk.'

'True.'

'And a mug cake isn't quite glamorous enough for Paris.'

'Agreed,' he said. 'Though, with a bit less sugar, it'd be nice.'

'Noted,' she said. 'Right. Tea and cake dispensed. Time for—maybe sympathy, but I think you're more the no-nonsense type. What happened?'

Maybe she was right and saying the words out loud would get them out of his head. None of the alternatives had worked yet, today. 'My brother,' he said, 'just had a baby.'

'And?' she asked, not quite understanding why Antoine would be upset about a new niece or nephew.

He looked away. 'With my ex.'

A baby.

His brother and his ex?

This was a complete minefield, and she wasn't quite sure what to say.

But Antoine clearly took the silence as waiting for him to speak, because he said, 'Of course I'm pleased for them.'

That wasn't what his face was saying. '*Are* you?' she asked.

'Yes. And no,' he admitted. 'I always thought Céline and I would get married and have children.'

Geri and Mark hadn't planned to have children. But then life had changed; and when she'd lost the baby they'd had a really honest conversation. One that had hurt both of them; Mark had been adamant that he still didn't want children, whereas the miscarriage had made her realise that her own feelings had changed.

That was one issue where there simply wasn't a middle way: one of them would've had to compromise and do something they really didn't want to. And finally, although it had made them both sad, they'd agreed that they needed to go their separate ways and find the life they wanted.

Had Antoine gone through something similar?

'I'll ask you the tough question,' she said. 'Why is she your ex?'

'Because she fell in love with my brother.' He blew out a breath. 'Neither of them wanted to hurt me. Jean-Luc even moved to Chartres, two hours away, to try and stay away from her—thinking he'd be able to forget her. And she thought she could make herself fall out of love with him.'

'But it didn't work?' she asked quietly.

'No. The morning of our wedding, she realised she couldn't go through with it.' The words tumbled out of him like pebbles churned up by the sea. 'My brother was my *témoin*—my best man, I guess he'd be in England. We were waiting outside the town hall, fifteen minutes before our slot. She called him, in tears. And he broke the news to me.'

Breaking Antoine's heart in the process.

'That's a really hard way to find out. And the timing was rough on you.'

'It could've been worse.' He shrugged. 'She could've actually stood next to me in the town hall, with all our close family and friends witnessing it, and then said no.'

But he would still have had to explain to everyone why the wedding was cancelled. 'Why didn't she say something to you before the day?'

'As I said, they thought they could fight their feelings. Neither of them wanted to hurt me. She thought she could go through with the wedding and save me being hurt.'

'And instead they hurt you very publicly.'

He inclined his head. 'We haven't spoken since. And I hate that my family feels they ought to take sides. It's my fault the family's split.'

'But you've done nothing wrong.'

'Jean-Luc and Céline didn't do it to be malicious. They're not the bad guys. I know that.'

'But there's a difference between know-ing something with your head, and knowing it with your heart,' she said.

He gave her a bleak look. 'The first step to any reconciliation will probably have to come from me. But making myself do it…' He shook his head. 'I don't expect my parents to refuse to see their first grandchild. I know they see Jean-Luc and I'm fine with that. He's their son, too. But, if I make it up with him… everyone's going to pity me. Especially now, with the baby. And I can't bear that.'

'Maybe,' she said carefully, 'they won't pity you.'

'Oh, but they will. Poor Antoine, whose fiancée fell in love with his brother.' He grimaced. 'That's not who I am. I'm a zoo vet. A good one.'

Was that the only way he saw himself—defining himself by his job? 'You're also *you*,' she said. 'Losing your brother and your fiancée, on what should've been a day to celebrate, must've been hard.' She reached out to squeeze his hand.

'It is what it is. But that's why I don't socialise much. I don't have the heart for it, any more.' He pulled away from her hand. 'And I don't enjoy being pitied.'

'I'm not pitying you,' she said. 'But I do think you're missing out, hiding yourself away in your shell.'

'You're saying I'm a tortoise now, rather than a panda?' He gave her a speaking look.

'No. Just…' She blew out a breath. 'I kind of know how you feel, because I've been there.'

'Your fiancé jilted you on your wedding day, too?' There was a slight edge to his tone, and she realised she'd gone too far. Maybe she needed to share some of her past, too.

'No. Mark and I got married.' She wasn't quite up to telling Antoine about the baby she'd lost, and the subsequent slow and painful unravelling of her marriage. 'It didn't work out. We found out the hard way that we wanted different things.' The shock of learning she was pregnant had quickly been replaced by unexpected joy; until then, she hadn't realised that she did actually want children. Though, thanks to the disease she'd caught, she might never be able to have children. 'So we got divorced. And let's say I've learned that life's better when I'm being what you called a little ray of sunshine—if I've translated that right?'

He winced. 'I apologise for being rude.'

She shook her head. 'I wasn't fishing for an apology. I simply meant that there's another way of dealing with a broken heart that might help you more than avoidance. It worked for me, anyway.' She spread her hands. 'Fake it until you make it.'

Ant rather thought his own solution worked better. Keeping himself separate from other people was the best way to keep his heart safe. No involvement meant no chance of getting hurt again. And staying away from his family—much as he missed them—meant he didn't have to face the guilt of knowing the split in his family was his fault. Because he couldn't get past it.

But she'd said that she'd been there. She knew the same dark places he did, and he'd seen a world of pain in her eyes when she'd said that she and her ex had wanted different things. Had her ex cheated on her? Or had something else caused the split?

'Your divorce—is that why you came to Paris?'

'Partly. It's why I switched to zoo medicine.'

'Was your ex a vet?'

'No. He was a dentist. We met in our last year at uni,' she said. 'At the time, we thought we were what each other wanted. But we both ended up focused on our careers and we let the spontaneity drain out of our relationship. So I wanted to do something different. I wanted to experience another culture and live in another country for a few months.'

'Hence your Paris list.'

'Yes. I'm happy to tick things off on my own, but sometimes it's more fun to do it with someone else.' She gave him a level look. 'This isn't me propositioning you, by the way. I'm not looking for a relationship. But a friend—I'd like that. And I could be your friend, too. If you'd like that.'

A friend.

Something felt as if it was cracking, somewhere in the region of where his heart used to be.

'I was thinking, maybe you could come with me. Show me the things in Paris I might've missed on my list, and I can maybe teach you to see the city with new eyes.' She smiled. 'You never really explore the place where you live unless you're showing it off to someone else.'

'I guess that's true,' he said.

Explore Paris with her.

Could he do that?

She'd accused him of being a tortoise, stuck in his shell. Maybe she was right. He knew his sister and his parents worried about him. Showing Geri round Paris might be a bigger step towards getting some sense of normality back in his life.

'We could,' she said, 'make a start tonight. Having a drink at the Moulin Rouge, and maybe go somewhere for a pizza.'

'The traditional *French* pizza, would that be?' he asked wryly.

'Obviously I know it's Italian. But pizza's my carb of choice when I've had a tough day,' she said. 'Which it sounds like you have.'

'Be prepared for the Moulin Rouge to be extremely touristy,' he warned.

'Bring on the can-can and the accordions,'

she said with a grin. 'I can even pretend to swish my skirt.'

He looked at her jeans. 'Pretend.'

'I own skirts,' she protested.

'If you want to see the show, you need to book,' he said.

'Maybe we'll do that another time, then.' She took her phone from her pocket. 'Or we could visit one of the bars where the artists used to drink.'

'I'd need to look them up, if you want to tour them,' he said.

'OK. I'll settle for the pizza,' she said.

'All right. I'll buy you dinner instead of cooking it,' he said. 'As your friend.'

'And, as *your* friend, I'll buy the wine.'

He'd let her argue that later. 'OK. We can go whenever you want.'

'I'm hungry now,' she said. 'Despite scoffing a mug cake. I've walked *miles* today. Do I need to dress up?'

'You're fine as you are,' he said. More than fine. Not that he was going to let himself think about how attractive Geri Milligan was. It wasn't appropriate, and his head wasn't in the right place; it wouldn't be fair to take this further, even if she felt the same attraction towards him.

Though the flickerings wouldn't go away.

His awareness of her. The way she smiled, the way her eyes seemed to change colour—almost like a spring afternoon sky, when she was happy. The way she challenged him, making him see things in a new light instead of leaving him to brood on his problems alone.

He took her to a small pizzeria not far from the apartment, and made sure that she had the seat with a view because he was pretty sure she'd enjoy it.

'The Sacré Coeur looks amazing from here,' she said, looking thrilled.

'I'll take you round it, another day,' he said. 'And maybe you can have your portrait drawn in charcoal by one of the artists. It's touristy, yes, but it's also kind of a rite of passage.'

'I'd love that,' she said.

Once they'd ordered their pizza and a couple of glasses of wine, he looked at her. 'Tell me about your Paris list. Not that having a list says spontaneity to me.'

'I'm going to be spontaneous about when I see them,' she corrected. 'The list is because I don't want to miss out on all the big things. I want to go to the Eiffel Tower—right to the very top—and I want to see it at night when it sparkles. And walk down the Champs-Élysées.'

'To go shopping?'

'Isn't it meant to be *the* shopping street in Paris?' she asked.

'It's a tourist trap,' he said, wrinkling his nose. 'If you want luxury shopping, go to la Rue de Faubourg Saint-Honoré. Most Parisians shop at la Rue du Commerce, near the Eiffel Tower, or in the Marais.'

She grabbed her phone and made notes. 'Got it. And I want to dance next to the Seine.'

He couldn't remember the last time he'd danced. 'We can do that,' he said. 'Though I'm a bit out of practice.'

'Everything I saw online said that it didn't matter if you were a beginner. And you *have* to do a tango in Paris, don't you? Or maybe salsa. Either will do.'

Perhaps it hadn't been such a good idea to agree to this; both dances were incredibly sensual. And he didn't dare let himself think about sensuality and Geri Milligan. 'Museums?' he said, trying to find a safer subject.

'I want to visit all of them,' she said gleefully. 'And all the art galleries. But I especially want to see the enormous Monet water lily paintings at the Musée de l'Orangerie. I missed them when three of them were exhibited in London.'

'We're both off duty on Sunday. I could drive you out to Giverny to see Monet's garden for yourself,' he suggested, and was rewarded with a smile that made the lingering shadows vanish.

'That's also on my list—but are you sure it's not too much trouble?'

'I'm sure,' he said. 'It's an easy drive. You're a big fan of Monet?'

She nodded. '*The Water Lily Pond* is my favourite painting in the whole world, and I'd love to see the actual pond he painted. I was planning to work out how to get to Giverny from Paris.'

'You can go by train, but I'll drive you and we can maybe see some of the area around Giverny, too,' he said. 'We'll book tickets tonight. Even if it's wet on Sunday, I have no doubt you'll see the sunshine.'

She narrowed those perceptive blue eyes at him. 'Are you laughing at me?'

'No, at myself,' he said. 'Because you're right. I'm used to being in my shell, in the darkness. Maybe I should try things your way. Look for the sunshine.' And fake it, if he had to. That had never occurred to him before. He'd simply blocked everything out, focused on his work and avoided social situations.

'Good,' she said.

After her first bite of pizza, she closed her eyes in apparent bliss. 'This is perfect. Proper thin-crust Italian pizza,' she said. 'And goat's cheese with rocket and chili jam is the *perfect* combination.'

She liked the wine, too.

And the limoncello ice cream he'd eschewed in favour of an espresso. 'This is amazing. You really have to try this, Antoine.'

'Call me Ant,' he said, shocking himself. He'd known Geri for three short days. He would never normally invite such informality on such a brief acquaintance. Maybe her spontaneity was catching.

'Ant,' she said with a smile, and proffered her spoon.

He shocked himself further by leaning over and actually letting her feed him the ice cream. 'It's a little sw—' He stopped himself mid-sentence. No negativity. 'It's nice,' he said.

But she'd clearly picked up on what he'd been about to say. 'Except you don't do sweet.

You like things sharp—like your breakfast marmalade,' she said.

He spread his hands. 'Sorry.'

'And to think I brought you chocolates and biscuits,' she said, looking rueful.

'It was a kind thought,' he said. 'Besides, I like dark chocolate.'

She grinned. 'Of course you do. *La nuage.*'

'It's *le*, not *la*,' he said, grinning back. 'And probably that should be *le nuage d'orage*—a storm cloud. Because of course we surly Parisians will always correct your grammar and your vocabulary.'

'Actually, joking apart, I *want* you to correct my grammar,' she said. 'It helps me learn. Anyway, you're not being surly, right now. You're smiling.'

'It's you,' he said, shocked to realise that it was true. Her company had made him feel composed again. 'Thank you. For taking the shadows away. I don't know how you did it.'

She gave him a look that made his blood heat. 'I believe it's what little rays of sunshine are supposed to do.'

Right at that moment, he wanted to pull her into his arms and prove to her that he did like sweet—at least, if it was going to involve kissing her. But that wasn't their deal. She'd

offered him friendship, and that was probably more than he deserved. 'Hmm,' he said,
and sipped his coffee.

CHAPTER FOUR

GERI CONTINUED TO enjoy her first week at the
zoo. Thankfully the okapi didn't need surgery—the X-ray showed that the problem was
an infection which would be easily cleared up
with antibiotics—but they did need to operate on a lemur who'd had a fight with another
lemur in the enclosure, and needed sutures
in the cut across his palm.

'Your stitching's very neat,' Antoine said
as she finished the last dissolvable stitch.

'It needs to be. I don't want to leave him a
place where he can open up that wound and
we have to restitch it,' she said. 'I've had to
do that before with a dog after I'd removed
a strawberry lump from her leg; the owners
didn't keep quite a close enough eye on her,
and she took the stitches out that evening.'

'Did you work mainly with small animals
before you switched to zoo medicine?' Antoine asked.

'No. Farm animals.' And she needed to head him off that subject. She didn't want to think about sheep—or the baby that would've been a toddler now. 'Once our lemur's round from the anaesthetic and recovered, what's next today?' she asked brightly.

'Bloods from Bianca,' he said. 'I'm keeping an eye on her kidneys.'

Geri knew that kidney disease, particularly in older animals, was one of the leading causes of death in tigers. 'How long has she had a kidney problem?'

'About a year,' he said. 'We noticed she was becoming a bit lethargic and spending less time outdoors, and her appetite decreased. The blood tests showed that she had kidney disease, but she's responded well to medication.'

Geri could see that Antoine was concerned, and she remembered him admitting that Bianca was his favourite animal at the zoo. 'How old is she?'

'She's fifteen now,' he said, 'which is nearly twice as old as she'd live to be in the wild. We're keeping a close eye on her and making sure she's comfortable—and that means regular blood tests to see how she's doing.'

Once the lemur was in recovery under

the watchful eye of his keeper, they headed for the tiger enclosure, where Antoine introduced her to Belle, the senior carnivore keeper. 'Belle's been training all the tigers so we can handle them for routine vaccinations, health checks and blood draws—we like to avoid anaesthetics where we can, to keep the risks lower,' he told Geri. 'And it's good that we can see their gaits close up if we're concerned there might be an issue with a paw or a muscle—they'll walk steadily up and down next to the glass, meaning we can study them, and they'll offer a paw or a belly if we need a closer look.'

'And you trained them to do all that?' Geri asked Belle.

'As part of the team, yes. It takes anything from a couple of months to a couple of years to get to that level, depending on the tiger,' Belle said. 'Obviously we can't go in with the big cats like you would with a pet dog. We train them by capturing their behaviour and using positive reinforcement. When they're sitting, we'll say "sit", use the bridge word of "good" so they have a sound to associate with what we want them to do, and give them a treat immediately. They pick it up pretty quickly. We work up to "down", "up" and "roll over"—it's mimicking natural behaviour rather than doing tricks to entertain visitors, because they'll roll in scent markers anyway. Training is good mental stimulation for our cats, too.'

'Enrichment's always a good thing,' Geri agreed.

Belle stood at the wire link fence and called, 'Bianca!'

'She comes to her name?' Geri asked, surprised.

'Wait and see,' Belle said with a smile.

A few moments later, the white tigress came over to them at the wire mesh and made a soft 'brr' sound.

'Hello, gorgeous girl.' Belle gave the tigress a chunk of meat on the end of a stick.

'Hello, Bianca,' Antoine said, and mimicked the 'brr' sound.

To Geri's amazement, the tiger made the noise again, as if she were talking back to Antoine. 'I thought they only chuffed like that to greet other tigers?' she asked.

'And to the keepers and people they know, here,' Antoine said. 'I guess that makes us honorary tigers.'

The slight glint of mischief in his eye told her that he remembered she'd said he was like a panda and a tortoise, the evening before. Now he was adding a third animal to the descriptions. He was definitely as wary as a tiger, she thought. But the fact that a wild animal clearly trusted him so much…did that mean maybe she could trust him with her innermost secrets and open up to him, the way he had with her?

'Bianca, down,' Belle said.

Bianca lay down at the command, exactly like a dog would, with her head facing Belle, and Belle gave her another treat. 'Good girl.'

The position meant that the tigress's tail was next to a small inspection hatch in the fence that Antoine could unlock; he used a snake hook to bring her tail safely through the gap, and again Geri admired the way he handled the animal, calm and confident. Antoine Bouvier was definitely the reliable type.

'Good girl, Bianca,' Belle said again, giving the tigress another piece of meat.

'She's really good about having the blood taken,' Antoine said.

'How do you train a tiger not to mind having bloods done?' Geri asked.

'We start by feeling the end of the tail gently, and then work all the way up from the end of the tail to the base,' he explained. 'When they're comfortable with that, we use a little bit of pressure with our fingertips; then we progress to using a small needle, and finally work our way up to a larger gauge—the sort for taking bloods.'

'We pay attention to how the tiger reacts to each change; if they twitch or flinch or walk away, we take it back a notch and keep trying until they're comfortable with the new procedure,' Belle added.

'And there's a command Belle didn't mention—"open". It means we can do a visual check of their teeth,' Antoine said.

He used alcohol on a wipe to disinfect the tigress's tail and felt for the vein; gently, he said, '*Poussée*, Bianca,' and Belle gave the tigress a treat as Antoine drew the blood sample.

'Good girl,' he said when he'd finished, and this time Antoine was the one to give her the treat at the end.

'That's really incredible,' Geri said. He clearly had a close bond with the tiger, and she couldn't quite get over the way the tiger had responded to him.

The tigress drew her tail back in through the inspection hatch, which Antoine closed behind her and then Belle locked it.

'All done,' Antoine said, and gave the tiger a final treat.

Bianca gave another soft chuff, then got to her feet and padded away.

'I really hope those bloods turn out to be the same as last time,' Belle said, looking worried. 'That she hasn't deteriorated even a little bit.'

'I know,' Antoine said. He gave Belle a sympathetic smile, then took a deep breath. 'I'm not ready to say goodbye to our old girl just yet, either.'

Belle's eyes glittered with tears. 'I wish…' She shook herself. 'I know we're not supposed to get attached to the animals. But how can we not? They're part of our family.' She gave a wry smile. 'Though I guess you wouldn't want a tiger weighing one hundred and fifty kilograms sitting on your lap like a tabby.'

'That's assuming you had a sofa big enough for a tiger to sprawl across in the first place,' Antoine said.

And, just for a moment, Geri could imagine the two of them sprawled on Antoine's sofa. How it would feel to lie in his arms, talking sweet nothings and stealing kisses… She shook herself. This was crazy. She couldn't let herself act on the attraction. And right now she should be focused on the tiger, not on Antoine.

'I'll let you know as soon as I get the results, Belle,' Antoine added.

He was quiet all the way to the lab, and Geri judged this wasn't the right time for small talk; he, too, was clearly worried about the tiger. He handed in the sample to the lab team and asked them to let him know when the results were ready, then turned to Geri. 'Time to check on the pandas.'

Both bears were back to their normal selves after the anaesthetic, and Pierre reported no change in Zhen's behaviour. There were no changes of hormones in her urine samples, either.

'Now we have to wait and see. The cub could arrive at any time in the next three to six months, if she did conceive on Tuesday,' Antoine said.

'I do hope it's not six months,' Geri said feelingly.

'If Zhen's definitely pregnant but hasn't given birth by the time your secondment ends, we'll sort something out to make sure you're here and you don't miss the birth,' Antoine said. 'Even if you have to take leave from your zoo.'

'Thank you.' She smiled at him. 'Having been there at the start of the procedure, I really want to be there at the end.'

'That's totally understandable,' he said.

'There was one thing I've meant to ask you

all week, but I forgot in the excitement of the pandas. Do I need to start looking for a flat myself, or is that something Marie's team will handle?' she asked.

'Marie's team should be sorting it out for you. But there's no rush for you to move out,' he said. 'I don't mind you staying. Actually, if you're settled here, I'm happy for you to stay for the whole six months.'

'Really? That's so kind. I'd like that. Thank you,' she said. 'Though I think I should pay you rent.'

'There's really no need. I don't have a mortgage,' he said. 'And I was thinking, too. It's said that one of the best ways to see Paris in the evening is on a river cruise. I could book us a slot for tonight, if you like; then you'll get to see all the major landmarks lit up. Sunset's at half-past eight; you'll see the City of Light at her best.'

'That'd be wonderful,' she said. 'I'd really like that.'

'Good. I'll book the tickets. Now, it's lunch-time for you,' he said, glancing at his watch, 'and I have some paperwork that needs sorting.'

'You're not going to join us?'

'No. Paperwork is a hazard of my job. It's fine. I'll eat a sandwich at my desk. But you need a break.' He ushered her towards the staff canteen.

Geri had to damp down the flicker of disappointment that he wasn't going to join her and the rest of the team for lunch, but she enjoyed chatting to Valerie, Émilie and Jacques. The rest of the afternoon was taken up doing rounds and treating minor issues, and then she met Antoine back at his office.

'Perfect timing,' Antoine said. 'We've got enough time to grab something to eat on the way to the boats.'

'How much do I owe you for the tickets?' she asked.

'It's fine. My treat.'

'Then I'll buy dinner,' she said. And, once they'd boarded the boat, she bought them both a glass of champagne. 'I'm seeing Paris by night for the first time. This deserves proper fizz,' she said.

This wasn't a real date; Antoine was simply joining her in the sightseeing. But, as Antoine clinked his glass against hers and said, *'Santé,'* her fingers brushed briefly against his and a frisson ran through her.

Oh, help.

She'd dated a few times, since the break-up of her marriage, but nobody had made her want to take the relationship any further than friendship. Antoine, both as her host and as her senior colleague, was off limits. Why did she feel this strange pull towards him? Why did she notice that, close up, there were little gold flecks in his dark eyes? Why did his smile make her feel as fizzy as the champagne they were drinking?

'Tell me what I'm seeing,' she encouraged him, wanting to be distracted from her thoughts.

'Right now we're going past the Île Saint-Louis,' he said. 'You can see Notre Dame on the next island; it isn't open for visitors yet, following the fire, but there's something on the Île Saint-Louis I'd like to show you later.'

'Any clues?'

'Something,' he said, 'I know you'll love.'

She groaned. 'Which tells me almost nothing.'

There was a glint of mischief in his eyes. Geri tried to tell herself that it was the sparkling wine making her feel slightly giddy, but she knew it wasn't: it was Antoine's nearness. For pity's sake. Neither of them needed any complications. She was here only for a few months, and he was clearly still nursing a broken heart after his fiancée dumped him on their wedding day.

He talked her through the history of the

opulent buildings of the Hotel de Ville, the city hall, as they went past. 'And you were here the other day,' he said as they reached the next building complex.

'The Louvre,' she said, enjoying the way the elegant façades were lit up.

'And there's Place de la Concorde. It's the biggest square in Paris,' he said. 'It's pretty now, with the fountains and the obelisk.'

She remembered what she'd read about the square. 'Isn't that where Marie-Antoinette…?' she began, then winced.

'And more than a thousand others.' He nodded. 'The obelisk was placed on the site of the guillotine.'

'It must have been terrifying in Paris during the Revolution,' she said.

'Not a time I would've liked to live through,' he agreed. 'There's the Petit Palais—you might want to add that to your list of art galleries, though it's worth a visit for the buildings themselves, if you like architecture.' He smiled. 'And now, on our left— something you've been waiting for.'

She looked up at the Eiffel Tower, all lit up in gold. 'It's amazing. With those lights, you can see how intricate the ironwork is.' She glanced at the top of the tower, where a beam of light stretched out across the city and swept round. 'I know it's touristy, but it's—oh!' she exclaimed in delight as the tower started sparkling. 'That's spectacular!'

'It sparkles like this for five minutes on the hour, every hour, until the tower closes to visitors a few minutes before midnight,' he said. 'The sparkling light show was originally set up for the Year 2000, and it was meant to be temporary, but it was so popular that the authorities decided to keep it.'

'I need to film this to show my family. Can I be rude?' She took her phone out and took a few seconds' video of the sparkling tower. 'This is even better than I expected.' And part of that was due to the company, though she didn't quite dare say as much.

As the boat went under another bridge, he said, 'This is the Île aux Cygnes.'

'Island of swans?' she checked.

'It's not named after actual swans, as far as I know,' he said. 'But there's something else famous here—the Statue de la Liberté.'

She blinked as she saw the statue. 'Like the Statue of Liberty in New York.'

'It's a quarter-size replica of the one that France gave to the United States,' he said. 'The United States gave this one to France to commemorate the centenary of the French Revolution.'

'I had no idea there was a Statue of Liberty in Paris.'

'Actually, there are seven of them,' he said, 'though this one's the biggest.'

She looked at him with narrowed eyes. 'Did you know that before this week, or did you look it up in a tourist guide?'

He laughed. 'Well spotted. As you said, you never get to know your own city until you show someone else round it. I checked out the points of interest on the river trip while I was eating my lunch, and a page came up talking about all the Statues of Liberty.'

Was researching touristy things the paperwork he'd referred to, earlier, rather than something for the zoo? Geri was touched that he'd made the effort, though part of her felt guilty that he hadn't had a proper break because of her.

'I made a list,' he said, 'in case you wanted to know about the others.'

'Yes, please,' she said.

He took out his phone, opened the notes app and handed the phone to her. Again, when his fingers touched hers, every nerve-ending in her skin tingled, and she nearly dropped the phone.

'Some of the places where you can find

them will already be on your list,' he said.
'The Musée d'Orsay, and the Eiffel Tower.'

'You're telling me there's a Statue of Liberty on the Eiffel Tower?' She smiled. 'I think you might be teasing me.'

'Not on the tower itself,' he said, 'but on a *péniche* nearby.'

'What's a *péniche*?' she asked.

'A houseboat or barge,' he said. 'And there's one Statue of Liberty on that list I'd like to see for myself because I had no idea it even existed—it's a tiny, tiny version peeping out of a centaur's breastplate on another statue.'

'Only in Paris,' she said.

'Only in Paris,' he echoed, and grinned.

When he wasn't being serious and looking slightly forbidding, Antoine was utterly gorgeous; that grin made her feel as if the whole evening had lit up.

'You can't quite see them from here, but I would definitely suggest adding the Jardins du Luxembourg to your list,' he said. 'Actually, all the parks in Paris are very pretty at this time of year, but that one's a bit special.'

'How would you recommend visiting everywhere I want to see?' she asked.

'We could break it down by arrondissement,' he said. 'Start at the first, and spiral out. Or buy a tourist map, ring everything you want to see and then make a list of places that are near to each other.'

'You work things out logically, then,' she said.

'It means you'll be able to make the most of your free time; but being organised doesn't mean that you can't still be spontaneous. I was thinking, we could visit something that's on your list, and then go off the beaten track and see what we find around it.'

'That sounds good to me,' she said. 'How long have you lived in Paris, Antoi— Ant?' she corrected herself, remembering that he'd given her permission to use the shorter version of his name.

'Since I was eighteen and came to study veterinary medicine.' He spread his hands. 'That's about fifteen years.'

Making him three years older than her, she calculated.

'I know some parts of the city much better than others—the fifth arrondissement because I lived there as a student, Montmartre because of my grandparents and obviously I live there now, and the tenth because I lived there after graduation.'

With his ex? Though it felt too crass to ask.

'What I found today intrigued me. I'm

looking forward to learning more about the city I don't know,' he said.

'You really don't have to do the super-touristy bits with me if you don't want to,' she said.

He spread his hands. 'This would count as super-touristy. I've never been on one of these cruises before, and I'm not sure I know anyone who has.'

She grimaced. 'Sorry.'

'No need to apologise. It's surprising, seeing bits of the city I thought I knew well but from a different angle,' he said. 'We can climb the Eiffel Tower—though it's your choice whether we walk up the steps to first stage or take the lift all the way. It's a bit of a trek.'

'Given that I plan to try crème brûlée in as many places as possible,' she said, 'I think I probably ought to walk up.'

'*D'accord,*' he said. 'And here's the Musée d'Orsay.'

'You can really see it used to be a railway station,' she said, looking at the beautiful building. 'And I love that clock.'

'If we go to the top floor, we can look out at Paris through the clock—it's an iconic view,' he said.

'I'd love that. And I can see why Paris is

called the City of Light—all the buildings are brightly lit, and I love the way the lights are all reflected in the Seine,' she said.

'As a surly Parisian,' he said, 'I need to correct you a little. It's actually because Paris was a centre of scientific ideas and enlightenment in the late eighteenth century.'

'Light and enlightenment,' she said.

'Though Paris was also the first city to introduce street lighting,' he said. 'And there are twenty thousand bulbs on the Eiffel Tower alone. I guess the popular view has a point.'

'Twenty thousand bulbs? No wonder it sparkles,' she said. 'But Paris is a beautiful city. Thank you very much for organising this.'

'My pleasure. I'm enjoying it, too.'

Later that evening, Ant sat in his study and thought about it. When Geri had suggested that he join her in sightseeing, saying that she could maybe teach him to see the city with new eyes, he'd been sceptical. But even the little bit they'd seen together tonight had felt different. He'd grown so used to the Eiffel Tower that he didn't really see it any more; but, thinking how much Geri might enjoy it, he'd chosen the cruise that would go past the tower on the hour and they'd see the sparkling up close. The delight on her face had been his reward; but he'd also seen the illuminations of the stunning Parisian icon through her eyes, as if for the first time, and it had felt magical.

Sipping champagne on a Seine river cruise was something he'd never thought of doing. If he was honest, he would probably have sneered at the suggestion as being something for tourists. But, with Geri, it had been different. Fun. Carefree. And it had felt as if the lights of the city had penetrated the dark cloud that was normally wrapped round him.

He was going to have to be careful. Geri was only here on secondment. She was his colleague, and his houseguest—even if it was only temporary. He couldn't risk acting on the attraction he felt towards her and getting involved with her as more than just her friend; there were too many barriers. He'd need to be really careful. *Sensible.*

On Friday and Saturday, they were both busy at the zoo, but they'd planned to visit Monet's house at Giverny on Sunday. Antoine had suggested going early, to miss most of the crowds, and drove them out to the little village where Monet had once lived.

'Do you like simply looking at art,' he asked, 'or do you sketch or paint?'

'I can barely draw a straight line with a ruler,' she said cheerfully. 'My worst times in class as a student were when I was asked to draw things. I'm glad I don't have to do that any more.' She smiled. 'What about you?'

'Drawing didn't worry me. Though my tutors all complained about my handwriting,' he admitted ruefully.

'Medics—human or otherwise—are *supposed* to have terrible handwriting,' she said. 'Do you like art?'

'Some,' he said. 'I'm not keen on the really abstract stuff. But I like Monet. There's something about the way he paints light and water that's really soothing.' He'd never really thought about that before; Geri was definitely teaching him to look at things in a different way.

'That's what I like about his paintings, too,' she said. 'I'm really looking forward to seeing the gardens. Apparently he planted like a painter rather than a gardener—he was way ahead of his time.'

'You like gardens?'

'My mum's a keen gardener,' she said. 'And she loves visiting stately homes, but she goes to see the gardens rather than the houses. Not to mention the Chelsea Flower Show. She watches every gardening programme going, and Alex—my little sister—and I buy her an annual membership to Kew Gardens and to the Royal Horticultural Society so she gets her garden fix whenever she wants to.' She smiled. 'She's hugely envious that we're going to Giverny. I need to take a million pictures of the tulips for her.'

Ant liked the fact that Geri seemed close to her family, though at the same time it made him feel guilty that he didn't let his own family as close as he knew they wanted to be. He didn't know the circumstances around Geri's divorce, but she didn't seem to let the sadness of a breakup affect her the same way that he had.

His own mother loved flowers, too. Maybe he should send her some, 'just because'. It might help to bridge the gap he'd put between them.

When he parked the car and they headed for the entrance to Giverny, Geri's eyes were sparkling and her face was all lit up. 'I'm looking forward to this,' she said.

'Me, too,' he said, surprised to realise that he was. He'd always thought of visiting gardens as a pastime for the middle-aged, but maybe he was wrong about that.

'The spring flowers here are meant to be amazing,' she said, 'and then in the summer there are roses and the water lilies will be out.'

It sounded as if she'd been torn between visiting now and visiting later in the summer. 'Maybe we can come back again when the roses and water lilies are out,' he suggested. 'On a weekday, when it'll be a bit less busy.'

'I'd really like that,' she said, and her smile made him feel warm all over.

Once inside the grounds, they headed for the water gardens first. They took the underpass to the other side of the road, and emerged to be greeted with purple azaleas in full flower.

'This is lovely,' Geri said.

Not only lovely, he amended mentally; it was an incredibly romantic setting, and the light in this part of the Seine valley seemed to have a special soft quality to it. The path went alongside a meandering stream, and the birds were singing their heads off. His hand brushed against hers, and a zing of anticipation went all the way through him. It would be all too easy to accidentally on purpose let his hand touch hers again, then for his fingers to curve gently against hers and slide up until he was holding her hand.

He managed to resist the temptation as they walked past the bamboos, hearing the stream bubbling and the wind swishing through the leaves. Then they turned a corner and the famous green Japanese bridge was right in front of them; the arches above the bridge were covered in gnarled ropes of wisteria, the leaves bright green and the flowers in bud, and the willow trees drooped next to the bridge.

Geri gave a sharp intake of breath; when he looked at her, he could see a tear running down her cheek. He took her hand and squeezed it. 'Are you OK, *mon petit rayon*?' The nickname—and the possessive—slipped out before he could stop them.

She sniffed. 'Sorry. They're happy tears. I can't believe I'm really here and actually seeing this.'

'Stand in the middle,' he said, 'and I'll go a little further along the bank and take your picture.'

She did as he directed, leaning on the bridge and smiling; for one crazy moment, it felt as if he was taking a touristy photo of his girlfriend, and he couldn't help wondering why her ex had let someone as lovely as Geraldine Milligan go.

Not that it was any of his business, he reminded himself, and went back to join her.

'I'll send the picture over to you later,' he said.

'Thank you. Do you want me to take one of you?'

'It's fine,' he said, smiling at her. 'Let's walk round the lily pond. The lily pads look like little islands—and I can't believe how clear the water is.'

She stopped every few metres to take pictures of the flowers surrounding the pond, the irises and tulips and little white pom-pom daisies.

At the far end of the pond, she took photographs of the bridge under the willows. 'That's going to be top of my social media pictures today,' she said happily.

Ant had teased Geri about being a little ray of sunshine, but that was exactly who she was, he thought. Her joy in her surroundings was infectious, and when they went back over into the main garden he could see the same magical things that she did.

'The whole garden's like a vast Impressionist painting. All those hundreds and hundreds of tulips—each one looks like a dot of paint on a canvas,' she said.

That would never have occurred to Ant before, but now she'd said it he could see it for himself. The tulips of all colours, the pansies and the daisies, together made up a whole that was more than their constituent parts. 'And those jonquils under the apple trees—they look like clouds drifting across the grass,' he said.

The air was sweet with the blossom of the cherry trees and apple trees, and everywhere was a riot of floral joy: a froth of forget-me-nots with bright red pops of tulips, and beds laid out like a painting box of whites and purples. The scent and the vision, combined with the birdsong, made him feel dizzy; he wanted to sweep Geri into his arms and kiss her until she was as dizzy as he was.

He managed to keep a grip on himself—just—and walked round the garden with her, letting her chatter about the flowers. But he still couldn't help wondering: *What if?*

Geri knew she was talking too much. But Giverny really was overwhelming to all the senses; the sound of the birds, the gorgeous colours of the flowers, the irresistible lure of touching some of the soft petals as she stooped to take a photograph for her mum, the scent of the blossom—so strong, in places, that she could practically taste it.

More than that, though, was Antoine's nearness.

When she'd been moved to tears by the sheer beauty of the bridge over the lily pond, he'd taken her hand and squeezed it to comfort her. His touch had made every nerve in her body shimmer, and she'd been oh, so close to turning towards him, wrapping her arms round him and resting her head against his shoulder.

This was exactly the kind of place where you'd walk hand in hand with the one you loved. Mark would've hated the way the plants spilled over the edges of their borders—if he'd visited a garden for a Sunday afternoon picnic with her family, he'd only really liked the super-formal type with box hedging and everything in its precise place. Despite his roof garden, she didn't think Antoine was the garden type, but he seemed to understand what she liked about this place: the light and the way the colours blended.

Her hand brushed against his several times as they walked through the gardens, and she had to make a conscious effort not to link her fingers with his. He'd been kind enough to drive her here, and he'd agreed to help her with her Paris list; but she knew that friendship was all he was offering. He clearly still wasn't quite over being dumped on his wedding day—an experience that would break anyone's heart but must have been so much harder for Antoine, given that his ex had fallen for his brother.

They walked under the wide archways where the roses would spill down in late summer, and headed for the house with its pink walls and bright green paintwork. Inside, the rooms were light and bright. 'I love this room,' she said when they walked into the bright yellow dining room. 'I could imagine living here.' She loved the kitchen next door, too, with the blue and white tiles on the wall in sharp contrast to the red floor and the copper pans hanging down from the shelf on their hooks. 'I could imagine cooking here—though I'm not sure I'd enjoy having to black-lead the range.'

'Actually, it's not that much of a chore,' he said. 'You simply squeeze out a bit of paste onto a rag, rub it over the cast iron, leave it to dry and then buff it with a shoe brush or a soft cloth.'

She blinked. 'Are you telling me *you've* black-leaded a range?'

He smiled. 'A fireplace, but it's the same technique. When we were small, the three of us used to help my grandmother's housekeeper. Obviously we ended up covered in the stuff, and she probably had to go round after us and do the bits we missed, but I remember it being fun. And then she'd bake us madeleines and we'd eat them warm from the oven.'

She smiled back. 'Very Proustian. I'm also a bit surprised you like them, given that cakes are sweet.'

'The ones we ate as a child were sweet. Nowadays, if I ate them, I'd choose very lemony ones, preferably on the sharp side,' he said.

She was glad that his childhood memories hadn't been ruined. Though she couldn't shift the fact that he'd talked about the three of them with such affection. 'Were you very close to your sister and brother when you were small?'

His expression clouded. 'It was a long time ago.'

'I can't imagine life without my sister in it,' she said. 'We fell out a few times, in our teenage years, but we always made up.'

'What happened between Jean-Luc and me was a bit more than a teenage squabble,' he said coolly.

'I know,' she said. 'If I were in your shoes— if Alex had fallen in love with Mark—I would've been really hurt and angry at first, but then I would've missed her dreadfully.'

'Even if she'd told you on your wedding day?' he asked.

She nodded. 'Alex is my best friend as well as my sister. We message or talk every single day we don't see each other.'

'Jean-Luc was my best friend, too,' he admitted. 'He trained as a vet. We were going to set up a practice together back in the Loire valley—he's three years older than I am—only I fell in love with zoo medicine. I told him how I felt, torn between wanting to support him and wanting to work in a different area, and he was the one who told me to follow my heart, apply to the zoo and stay in Paris.'

'Do you miss him?' she asked softly.

If anyone else had asked him that question, Ant would've given an abrasive reply. But with Geri it felt natural to talk about Jean-Luc. Because she was a stranger? Or because there was a connection developing between them? 'Yes, I do,' he admitted finally. 'I used to follow him about when I was small—as did Mélie. We called ourselves the Three Musketeers, and one of the vineyard dogs would be co-opted as D'Artagnan. Or one of the cats, if the dogs got bored.'

She took his hand and squeezed it; this time, Ant realised it was a touch of support, not of pity, and he didn't pull away.

'And you haven't seen him or talked to him since the day he left?' she asked.

'No.' He blew out a breath. 'I don't even know where to start.'

'New baby, new start?' she asked. 'I know she's the baby you should've had—but, the way I see it, babies are there to be treasured by everyone.'

There was an odd note in her voice, as if she was trying to be brave about something. But, before Ant could ask her, she added, 'And I bet he misses you just as much. Plus he must feel guilty about hurting you in the first place, and worrying that he'll hurt you even more if he makes the first move—or that you'll reject him.'

That hadn't occurred to Ant before— that Jean-Luc might be scared of rejection. 'Maybe,' he said. But he needed time to think about it a bit more. 'Shall we look at the next room?'

The expression on her face told him that she knew he was avoiding the subject—but also that she understood.

* * *

Once they'd seen everything in the house and Geri had bought some seeds for her mum and postcards in the gift shop, they took a last wander round the lily pond, and then made a detour to the nearby town of Vernon.

They ate a quick lunch of a galette with a green salad in a bistro overlooking the Old Mill—a half-timbered building straddling two piers of the ancient bridge—and when Geri looked it up on her phone she was delighted to discover that Monet had painted it.

'Now for some spontaneity,' Antoine said. 'Shall we see where the road takes us?'

It turned out to be a ruined castle, with amazing views of the Seine valley, and Geri enjoyed every second exploring with Antoine.

Back in Montmartre, he said, 'I can cook for us. Or we can go in search of crème brûlée.'

'Did you have somewhere in mind?'

'I do,' he said.

It was a small traditional bistro in one of the cobbled squares; inside, there were small tables covered with checked red and white tablecloths, bentwood chairs, and framed paintings of Montmartre on the walls. Better still, there was a grand piano in the centre of the room, and they were treated to live music. Best of all, crème brûlée flavoured with orange blossom was on the menu.

'This is perfect—it's so Parisian,' she said.

He looked pleased. 'I'm glad you like it. By the way, do you know where the word "bistro" comes from?'

'No. Enlighten me,' she said.

The glint in his eyes told her he realised she was riffing on their conversation about the City of Light, and appreciated it. 'It's probably an urban legend but, during the war with Russia in 1814, the Cossack soldiers used to shout "bistro"—or at least something that sounded like it—to make the waiters hurry up with their drinks.'

'Good story,' she said. 'I thought it'd be called after a particular dish or something like that.'

'Or a *bistraud*, an assistant wine-seller,' he said.

This was yet another side of Antoine: the urbane Parisian who took delight in word-play. The more Geri got to know him, the more she liked him.

The steak frites were good, but the dessert was perfect. 'Is this the best crème brûlée in Paris?' she asked.

'I wouldn't know,' he said. 'But my grandmother always ordered it here. I'd guess it's one of the best.'

'I'm definitely bringing my sister here,' she said. 'Although it would be rude not to try other places.'

He laughed, and she couldn't take her eyes off him. When he was relaxed like this, Antoine was mesmerising.

'I've really enjoyed today,' she said when they got back to his apartment.

'So have I,' he said.

She was pleased that he didn't use the excuse of paperwork to back away; instead, they ended up chatting about films they'd both enjoyed. And although she'd only known him for a week, it felt like much longer.

Paris, she thought, had been one of her better decisions.

CHAPTER FIVE

IF ANYONE HAD told Ant a few days ago that not only would he be happy to join his houseguest in visiting tourist attractions in Paris, he'd actually suggest some himself, he would've scoffed.

But here he was, leaving work at a normal time on a Monday afternoon instead of finding an excuse to stay at his office or double-check on a sick animal he'd already seen earlier that day, simply because it stopped him going back to an empty apartment and brooding. And it was all because of Geri and her 'fake it until you make it' idea: because he was quickly discovering that she was right. She'd helped him remember that he lived in one of the most beautiful cities in the world, one full of light and pretty parks and stunning architecture. More than that, she'd made him realise he could still feel that frisson of attraction—something he'd thought he'd lost when Céline had left him.

That evening, they went to the Parc Monceau and its pond with the beautiful colonnade, before visiting the Arc de Triomphe to watch the daily ceremony of the flame of remembrance being rekindled on the Tomb of the Unknown Soldier, after wreaths were laid by veterans.

'It's good to pay respects,' she said softly, when the ceremony had ended. 'And something like this makes me count my blessings. How lucky I am not to have lost someone I loved to war.'

He'd never really thought about that before. 'Yes,' he said.

They climbed the spiral staircase to the top of the arch. 'Twelve roads leading off one roundabout?' she asked, looking at the traffic. 'I'd imagine driving round this roundabout is an experience.'

'That's one word for it,' he said wryly. They lingered at the top and he pointed out some of the buildings she'd already visited, and others that he knew were on her list. Then they strolled down the Champs-Élysées, window-shopping and people-watching, before grabbing a bite to eat and giving Geri a chance to try more crème brûlée.

'It's nice—but not quite as good as the one I had at the weekend in Montmartre,' was her verdict. 'I think that one's going to be my benchmark.'

'It's a tough job, finding the best dessert,' he said. 'I probably ought to point out all the different Parisian specialities you're missing with this insistence on crème brûlée.'

'You could,' she said, 'but it's my sister's favourite, and it's my sworn duty to find her the best one in Paris. I'm being a Knight of the Round Table.' She gestured to the table they were sitting at—which was indeed round.

It was utterly ridiculous, but she made him smile. 'I give in,' he said. 'The quest for the crème brûlée continues…'

On Tuesday, at the usual morning meeting going through the daybook, Belle brought up the subject of one of the tigers. 'I was doing some routine training with Sabu yesterday afternoon, and I noticed a crack in one of his canines.' She handed her phone to Ant. 'I got Rico to take the snap while I asked Sabu to do an "open".'

'Is he eating normally? Is he showing any signs of pain?' Geri asked.

'He's eating normally,' Belle confirmed, 'and he doesn't seem in pain.'

Ant made a note. 'But this isn't something we want to leave,' he said, 'because I don't want to risk that tooth breaking nearer to the gumline and him ending up with an infection. Can you send me the picture? I'll send it over to Léa—the dentist,' he explained quickly to Geri, 'and talk to her about it this morning. Then we'll decide the action plan.'

'OK. Sending it now,' Belle said.

'Got it,' Antoine said, a couple of moments later. 'I'll send it to Léa before I do the rounds.'

Once they'd finished going through the daybook, Antoine shared out the tasks and sent the information over to the dentist. He'd almost finished checking on a frog with a lacerated leg when Léa called back to discuss the case.

At lunchtime, he went in search of Belle; luckily, as she was with Geri, he didn't have to find her afterwards and repeat himself.

'Léa's had a look at the photo,' he said, 'and she recommends doing a root canal filling and repairing Sabu's tooth. She can fit us in tomorrow. It's the usual drill for anaesthetics.'

'No food or drink after six o'clock this evening,' Belle said, 'and keep him separated from the others overnight.'

'Perfect,' Ant said. 'Geri, I'll need you to

help with the operation tomorrow morning. Can I put you on airway management?'

'Of course,' she said. 'Does Léa work only on animal dentistry?'

'Human as well,' Ant said. He remembered what she'd said about her ex being a dentist, but it wouldn't be kind to bring that up in front of someone else. Though he brought it up later that evening. 'You said your ex was a dentist. Did he work on animals as well as humans?'

Geri shook her head. 'We never worked together. Mark wasn't a big fan of animals.'

'Forgive me for being rude, but I don't understand why someone not keen on animals would even date a vet, let alone marry one.'

She nodded. 'With hindsight, I agree. But I suppose I always assumed that eventually we'd have children and get a dog and a cat.'

'You didn't talk about it?'

'We did. Neither of us wanted pets when we met—we were in our last year at uni— and it wouldn't have been fair to have a dog or cat when we were both working long hours.' There was a tiny pause. 'We thought we didn't want children, either.'

She'd said before that she and her ex had wanted different things. He saw the little flicker of pain in her expression, and it made him wonder what had happened. Had she realised later that, actually, she did want children, but her ex hadn't changed his mind? But before he could ask anything else, she switched the subject to the tiger's operation.

He understood where she was coming from. Talking about the past made you wonder where it had all started going wrong—and how could you be sure it wouldn't go wrong if you tried being close to someone in the future?

On Wednesday morning, they made an operating table with hay bales and a tarpaulin in the enclosure next to Sabu's. 'I don't know how you do things in Cambridge, but it's easier to work on him here—plus there isn't a table big enough in the operating theatre complex, and also it means less time under anaesthetic,' Ant said.

'We do the same with the larger animals,' Geri said.

Léa, the dentist, arrived, and Ant introduced her to the team.

With the help of Belle, Sabu lay down to let Antoine anaesthetise him through the mesh wall.

'We're going to put bubble wrap mittens on him,' Ant said, 'because he can't regulate his own temperature during anaesthesia. We'll put a duvet on him as well.' Ten minutes after Sabu had gone under, he checked the tiger's level of anaesthesia. 'OK. Ready to intubate, Geri.'

Geri sprayed the tiger's throat, made sure his jaws were kept safely open so they wouldn't snap shut on the oxygen tube—or the dentist's hand—then skilfully intubated Sabu and listened to his chest. 'OK, I'm happy,' she said. 'Ready to move him.'

Ant appreciated her professional approach and lack of fuss. 'Let's go,' he said.

It took four of them to move the two-hundred-kilogram tiger safely to the table. Belle and one of the other keepers put the bubble wrap mittens on the tiger and covered him with the duvet, and then Léa began the operation.

'This is the closest I've ever been to a tiger, and I've never seen dental work done,' Geri said. 'I can't believe how long those canines are.'

'About ten centimetres,' Léa said. 'And the root's up to six times longer than it is in a human tooth. Do you want me to talk through what I'm doing?'

'Yes, please,' Geri said.

'OK. I'm going to take off the tip of the

tooth, then remove the pulp and bacteria in the chamber of the middle of the tooth before packing it with inert material, then repairing the tip.'

Ant had seen similar procedures done, but it was still fascinating.

Geri kept a careful eye on the tiger's airway and stats, while Valerie recorded everything; and Ant kept an eye on the anaesthetic. The dentistry took three-quarters of an hour, and overall Sabu was under anaesthetic for two hours; there was a fine line between giving him enough anaesthetic that he didn't wake up during the operation, but not enough to stop him waking up again afterwards.

Once Léa had finished repairing the tooth, the team carried Sabu back to the enclosure and laid him on a bed of fresh straw; Geri removed the intubation and Ant reversed the anaesthesia. Within minutes, the tiger was back on his feet—a little bit wobbly, but able to walk over to the water trough.

'We'll do the usual post-anaesthesia protocol,' Belle said. 'We'll keep him on his own in the enclosure for the next twenty-four hours and monitor him one-to-one.'

'Any concerns, even if it's the middle of the night, call me,' Ant said.

* * *

By the middle of Thursday, Sabu had completely recovered from the operation and was eating and behaving normally again; Antoine and Belle were happy to let him re-join the other tigers in the main enclosure.

On Friday, Geri and Antoine had a day off, and they headed to see the Monets at the Musée de l'Orangerie and the Musée D'Orsay.

It was as wonderful as she expected; but Ant surprised her when they stopped to admire van Gogh's *Starry Night Over the Rhône*. 'I love this painting,' she said to Antoine. 'It's much more peaceful than the other *Starry Night*. Here, it feels like a beautiful evening and he's caught the joy of the sparkling stars and the lights from the building reflected in the water.'

'That's very you,' he said. 'Seeing the sparkle.'

His smile made her catch her breath; he was definitely paying her a compliment rather than being snippy. Did that mean he was starting to see her as something other than his colleague or his friend? she wondered. Because she was definitely starting to feel that way about him—even though it was risky and the idea of trusting her heart to someone again terrified her. She knew Antoine wanted children; so did she. But what if she couldn't have them? The Q fever that had caused her miscarriage made everything that much more complicated. It was the thing that had stopped her moving on, and she still didn't know how to get past it.

She smiled back and kept the conversation light until they got to the top floor, where they found the clock and admired the views of Paris. Antoine was taking a snap of her by the huge glass clock when a tourist asked, 'Would you like me to take a picture of you and your partner together?'

Partner. Did they look like a couple? Could they be a couple? The possibility made all her senses hum. She liked Antoine—she more than liked the man she was getting to know—but did he feel the same? She glanced at him, only to see that he looked as flustered as she felt. Better to be sensible, then.

'We're just good friends,' she said with a smile, 'but yes, please.'

Just good friends.

Ant was shocked to realise that they *were* actually becoming good friends. He felt relaxed in Geri's company, and he enjoyed their differences as well as their similarities.

He liked her calmness and common sense as a colleague, and the way she found the lightness in things.

He stood next to her with his arm round her shoulders and smiled for the camera. Holding her close like that felt unexpectedly natural, particularly when Geri relaxed against him. He could feel the warmth of her skin against his, smell the light sweet scent of her perfume, and for a moment it made him feel dizzy.

When was the last time he'd posed for a simple photograph?

It was unsettling, like it had been when he'd taken that snap of Geri on the bridge at Giverny and it had felt like taking a picture of his girlfriend. He hadn't dated since Céline had called off their wedding, and he didn't think he was ready to date anyone. But, if he did, he rather thought it would be someone like Geri Milligan.

Who was he trying to kid? He knew perfectly well it would be Geri herself. He liked her. He was attracted to her. But, although she was friendly and sweet and kind, he knew she believed in faking it until you made it. Her smiliness definitely hid something that she wasn't prepared to share with him. And he didn't have a clue how she really felt about him. How to get her to open up.

She nudged him. 'Hey, Monsieur le Nuage.'

He blinked. 'What?' Her phone was back in her hand, and he'd clearly been wool-gathering while she'd thanked the tourist for taking the snap.

'You're scowling.'

'Uh—I… Sorry.'

'Is it that bad, having your photograph taken?'

'No.' He stared at her, suddenly realising what she'd said. 'Did you just call me…?'

She grinned. 'Well, hey. You call me *le petit rayon*.'

'That's fair.' He couldn't stop himself smiling back. But at the same time, it made him think. If she was sunshine and he was clouds…did it mean they were too different for anything to happen between them?

And why was he thinking about dating, anyway? That wasn't what she'd agreed to. She'd agreed to be his friend. And he needed a friend more than he needed a romance—didn't he? Except Geri was the first person he'd really connected with in two years. Someone he felt able to open up to. And he wanted more.

'You're thinking again, Ant,' she said softly. 'Stop. Just *be*. Or do you need coffee?'

'I'm a Parisian. Of course I need coffee,' he said, glad of the excuse to change the soundtrack in his head. 'Actually, if we can get a table, how about having lunch somewhere famous—where Picasso, Hemingway and Sartre used to hang out?'

'That sounds great,' she said.

After a *croque monsieur* and coffee at Les Deux Magots—though, to Geri's regret, no crème brûlée—Antoine led her through to the Latin Quarter. 'It's the second-oldest district in Paris,' he said.

'Where does the name come from?' she asked.

'The university—because the lessons were all in Latin,' he said.

'And this is where you were a student?'

'Yes.' He took her through one narrow cobbled street and pointed to a tall building. 'I used to live on the top floor. My room was the third window from the left.' He smiled. 'The roof leaked whenever it rained, and it was way too hot in summer, but I have happy memories—and I'm still friends with my old flatmates.' Though he'd made excuses not to see them, too, since the mess of his wedding day, and lately they'd given up inviting him out.

'You didn't live with your grandparents?'

He wrinkled his nose. 'Grandmère and Grandpère did offer to let me live with them, because it would save me money, but I wanted to be like all the other students.'

'I get that,' she said. 'I would've been the same. Though it's pretty round here—all those tall windows and their wrought-iron balconies stuffed with plants, the blossom on the trees, and the little bistro tables under the awnings outside the cafés. It's nothing like my student accommodation. We had soulless modern blocks.'

'We have student accommodation like that in Paris, too,' he said. 'But the people you meet make the worst flats bearable.' He'd forgotten that. She'd helped him remember: and maybe he could help her, too. 'Were you in the same hall of residence as your ex?'

She shook her head. 'One of my friends was in a band with one of his friends. We met while we watched them play in a tiny room above a pub, and when we all went for chips afterwards Mark and I ended up talking for hours in the park. It was kind of like being instant soul mates.' She looked sad. 'But things change. Were you at university with Céline?'

'No. We met at a party—a friend of a friend kind of thing.' He lifted one shoulder. 'I'd split up with someone a couple of months before, but I just clicked with Céline.' He blew out a breath. 'Maybe if she'd met Jean-Luc before I asked her to marry me… But he was spending a year in America at the time. He was polite to her when he met her, but I never really noticed that he kept his distance from her, or that he tended to see me on my own and made excuses not to see us as a couple.' He rolled his eyes. 'Which makes me as clueless as that guy in *Love Actually*. Not that Jean-Luc would have done that horrible thing with the cue cards.'

'It sounds as if they tried to keep apart,' Geri said. 'Have you thought any more about going to see them?'

'I'm still thinking about it,' Ant said. 'I don't even know where to start.'

'Maybe send them a card,' she suggested. 'It will break the ice.'

'I still need to get my head round it,' Ant said.

'In your shoes, I would, too, Geri admitted.

'You can't change the past,' he said. 'And I'm not still in love with Céline.' He glanced at her. 'What about you? Are you still in love with Mark?'

'No. He's met someone else. They're happy—and they want the same things out of life, so I think it will stay that way.

So she wasn't still in love with her ex; and Ant was slightly shocked to feel the rush of relief that her heart wasn't engaged elsewhere. 'What about you?' he asked. 'What do you want from life?'

'That's a bit deep for a sunny Friday afternoon in Paris,' she said lightly. 'Actually, what I want from life right now is an ice cream.'

The determined look in her eye made it clear that she wasn't going to tell him any more right now; but at least she was starting to open up to him. 'Good call,' he said, 'because we're near somewhere I think you'll enjoy.'

They headed back to the river, and crossed over to the Île Saint-Louis.

'This is one of the oldest ice cream shops in Paris,' he told her when they reached their destination, 'and I happen to like their sorbet *cacao amer*.'

'Chocolate?'

'Bitter chocolate,' he said.

She grinned. 'Of course. Intense and dark.' Like him. 'As you bought lunch, the ice cream's on me. What do you recommend?'

'Ask the assistant for tastes of the ones you like the look of,' he said.

She ended up choosing salted caramel.

'Try this one, first,' he said, and offered her a taste of his sorbet. Time seemed to slow down, even stop, as he leaned forward with the teaspoon and watched her close her eyes in anticipation, and then her lips parted.

There was still a tiny speck of ice cream on her lips, and it would be oh, so easy to lean forward and kiss it from her mouth…

He went hot all over when she made a tiny hum of appreciation and opened her eyes again to look at him.

'How was it?' he asked, hoping that she couldn't guess what had just been going through his head.

'Intense,' she said.

'Too bitter for you?'

'Perhaps,' she said, and then took another taste of her own. 'But this is definitely one of the best ice creams I've ever had.'

It was the perfect day discovering the city, finishing up in a tiny bistro in the Latin Quarter that Antoine claimed served the best cassoulet in Paris. When they finally got back to Antoine's apartment, she was shattered.

'I've had such a brilliant day,' she said. 'Thank you.'

'My pleasure.'

She yawned. 'Sorry. It's all the walking. And the amazing food.'

'And you have crème brûlée from the bistro for dinner tomorrow.'

Because Antoine had persuaded the waiter to let them take dessert home, on condition they brought the dishes back.

'Breakfast,' she said. 'I can assure you it's not going to last until dinner.'

'You English heathen,' he teased.

She was delighted that he'd relaxed enough with her to be comfortable teasing her; she knew he didn't mean the insult in the slightest. At the same time, she had to make a real effort to stop herself leaning over and kissing that grin from his face.

Friends and colleagues. That was the deal, she reminded herself.

But what if…?

CHAPTER SIX

OVER THE NEXT few weeks, Geri really felt that she'd settled in to life in Paris. Thanks to Antoine, Valerie, Émilie and Belle, her French had come on in leaps and bounds and she was more confident in conversation. She'd explored lots of Paris with Antoine. And she was loving her days at the zoo, because Zhen was starting to show nesting behaviour—and her urine samples showed that she might be pregnant.

'Remember, the hormone changes are the same in a pseudopregnancy, so we can't rely on them,' Antoine warned. 'Until we persuade Zhen into letting us do an ultrasound—and the foetus, being tiny, is easy to miss—we can't be sure she's having a cub.'

'And in the meantime we monitor the progesterone levels in her urine every day,' Geri said. 'When they return to baseline, either she'll have the cub or we'll know she wasn't pregnant in the first place.'

But Zhen continued to be less active than usual, and they noticed that she was licking her body and cradling things: all behaviour that was linked to pregnancy.

'We'll build her a den in her off-show area,' Pierre said. 'In the wild, she'd nest in a cave with a bed of twigs, or in the hollow of a co-nifer tree—something small and very cosy. Though she'll always have access to the larger enclosure.'

'Are we telling the public that we're hopeful she's having a cub?' Geri asked.

'We're negotiating that one with the PR team,' Antoine said. 'Of course we want visitors to know things that will bring them to the zoo—but the welfare of the animals comes first, and I don't want her to be crowded.'

'Which is why,' Pierre said, 'we're putting her den in the off-show area so we can keep her relaxed. We'll add a bit of insulation to reduce noise, and we'll rig up a camera so we can monitor her and share some of the feed with visitors.'

'D'accord,' Antoine said.

* * *

Geri sat on the terrace of Antoine's roof garden on her afternoon off and video-called her sister.

'You,' Alex said, 'are absolutely glowing. Paris suits you.'

'I love Paris,' Geri said. 'And I can't wait until you come over. There are so many places I want to show you.'

'Places that you've been to with Antoine?' Alex asked.

'Yes. He's been helping me with my Paris list.'

'Is that what you're calling it?' Alex teased.

'I have no idea what you mean,' Geri fibbed.

'Yes, you do. You've gone pink,' Alex said with a grin. 'And do you have any idea how often you mention his name in conversation?'

'Because he's my colleague and my friend,' Geri protested.

'I think,' Alex said, 'you'd like him to be more than a friend.'

Geri felt her face heat even more. 'Not going to happen. He's my colleague—my *senior* colleague—and I'm staying with him.'

'He's single and you're single, right?' At Geri's nod, Alex continued, 'And he likes you, or he wouldn't be spending time with you. If you like each other, what's the issue?'

'It's complicated.' Geri didn't want to break Antoine's confidence, even to her sister.

'Geri, give yourself a break. Losing the baby and then splitting up with Mark broke you into little pieces. You deserve to have some fun,' Alex said. 'Mark's found happiness. It's *your* turn.'

'I know.' But Antoine was vulnerable, too. She didn't want to risk hurting him.

'Think about it,' Alex advised. 'If you like him and he likes you… Have a mad fling.'

'I'll think about it,' Geri said. 'Now, I want to hear all about *your* date, last night.' She smiled. 'And you look glowing, too.'

'You seem a bit out of sorts today,' Geri said the following day, when she and Antoine had left the zoo and were heading back to Montmartre.

'I am. Bianca's latest bloods aren't great, and I'm worried about her kidneys,' he said with a sigh.

'I'm sorry,' she said.

'I hoped that tweaking her meds would help, this week, but it hasn't.' He looked bleak. 'I haven't got it in me to tell Belle today, but I think we're going to have to make a hard decision in the next few weeks. For now, all we can do is to keep her comfortable.'

She squeezed his hand briefly in a gesture of sympathy.

'When I started training as a vet, I realised I didn't want to work in small animal practice, because I didn't want to have to break the news to an owner that their beloved dog, cat or rabbit couldn't be helped.' He looked away. 'Although zoo animals don't have an owner in the same way, the keepers grow attached to them as much as they'd be attached to a pet.'

'So do the vets,' she said. 'And the animals are just as attached to you. I still can't get over the way Bianca chuffs at you as if you're another tiger.'

'Yeah.' He bit his lip. 'I can't imagine the zoo without her. We came here on the same day. I mean, I don't ever want her to suffer— that's why I've been keeping a close eye on her bloods—but she's going to leave such a big hole in my life.'

'Of course she is,' Geri said. This time, she took his hand and kept hold of it, hoping to comfort him. Antoine had shut himself away from everyone after his breakup with Céline; he'd definitely started to open up and make those connections again since Geri had known him, but would Bianca's death set him back? 'But you're always going to have your memories,' she said. 'They're never going to fade.' A line of poetry drifted into her head. '"But thy eternal summer shall not fade."'

'Eternal summer. I like that,' he said. 'And you're right. I've got memories.'

'And you gave her a happy life, you and the keepers,' she reminded him. 'All the enrichment stuff you've read up on and shared with the keepers—and you kept Bianca healthy and safe.'

'Is that what you said to your farmers, when they lost a cow or what have you?' he asked.

'I've seen hard-bitten farmers in tears when a lamb or a calf hasn't made it, or when they've had to say goodbye to a sheep they've hand reared,' she said. 'So, yes. Even though it's a business and the animals aren't pets, there's still affection there. Which is how it should be—I'd hate to be in a world that doesn't have room for love.' She paused. 'I know it doesn't come easy to you, but promise me you'll talk to me rather than close yourself off?'

He was quiet for so long that she thought she'd gone too far.

And then he smiled. '*Mon petit rayon*. You have a generous heart. All right. I promise.'

'Good.'

'When does your sister plan to visit?' he asked.

'In July,' she said.

'She's very welcome to stay at the apartment,' he said.

She hadn't expected him to offer, but was delighted that he had. 'That's very kind of you, Ant.'

'*De rien.*' He looked slightly embarrassed. 'So you're close to your sister?'

'Yes. I'm really glad I can video-call her, because I miss her,' Geri said. 'Even though we see each other mainly at weekends, or when we both have a day off—Alex lives in London,' she explained, 'we talk most days. And she kept me going when I split up with Mark. Without her pushing me to do her classes, I think I would have just stayed indoors and shut—' She grimaced, suddenly realising what she was saying. 'Sorry. That wasn't a comment about you.'

'But it was pretty much what I did,' he said. 'Shutting myself away from everyone. Including my family, because it wasn't fair to make them choose between Jean-Luc and me.'

'Maybe they don't have to choose,' she said. 'Maybe they can still love both of you.'

'I think,' he said slowly, 'if my grandparents were still here, they'd urge me to reconcile. My grandmother always said how glad she was that the three of us were close. And there was no jealousy between us. I have the apartment, Mélie has a share of the vineyard, and Jean-Luc inherited investments. It was always fair.' He paused. 'Maybe you're right and I should send them a card. A gift for the baby.'

'It might be a good start,' she said. 'The baby's, what, six weeks old now?'

'You think it's a little too late to send something?'

'Your circumstances are different,' she said. 'I'd be at my sister's side for a cuddle at the first possible moment.' A cuddle with a baby who might end up being the only child in her life.

'As you say, my circumstances are different.' He sighed. 'It's weird. Of course I want to get to know my niece. If my brother had fallen for anyone else but Céline, I would feel the same way you do. But there's all this *stuff* in the way.'

'Maybe,' she said, 'you need to push it aside, because it's not helping you. If anything, I think it's hurting you more. I know it must feel like a horrible betrayal—no, it *was* a horrible betrayal—but do you want it to get in the way and suck out all the potential joy of the future?'

'No,' he said. 'But how do I push it away?'

'Fake it until you make it,' she said. Even though she knew she was a fraud, because she hadn't really made it, had she? 'In your shoes, once I'd stopped being hurt and angry, I think I'd miss them.'

'I do.' The words sounded as if they had been dragged through sand.

'Sending something's a good first step,' she said. 'As I said before, it'll help break the ice. Take it slow—like when you and Belle and the team train a tiger to sit and not mind you taking a blood sample.'

'Maybe I could buy the baby a toy tiger,' he said.

'That'd be nice, given what you do. A plush tiger sounds great,' she said. 'Or maybe a mobile with wooden animals on it to hang above the crib.'

'Perhaps you could come shopping with me at the weekend and help me choose something?' he suggested.

Choose something for a baby.

Panic flooded through her. Then again,

she'd just told him to push aside the hurt and stop it sucking out the joy of the future. Wasn't she making the same mistakes that he was?

That smile was definitely overbright.

'What's wrong?' Ant asked.

'Nothing,' she said.

He realised they were still holding hands—strange how natural that felt—so he tightened his fingers gently around hers. 'I think there is,' he said quietly. 'Talking to you helped me. Why don't you try talking to me? I'm not going to gossip, and I'm certainly not going to judge you,' he added. 'It might help.'

'I...' She was silent for a long, long time. And her voice cracked when she said, 'I had a miscarriage.'

And he'd just asked her to go shopping with him to choose things for a baby. Talk about trampling on a sore spot—though he'd had no idea. 'I'm sorry,' he said. 'That must've been tough. For your husband, too.'

'Mark was...relieved, I guess,' she said.

The words were so shocking, he wasn't sure he'd heard her right. 'Relieved?'

'He didn't want children.'

And he hadn't wanted pets, Ant remembered.

'He wouldn't ever have wished me to lose the baby—he isn't one of the bad guys, Ant. But he had a rough childhood, and it made him dead set against the idea of having children of his own. I thought I was OK with that, until I found out I was pregnant. It turned out I wasn't, because once I'd got over the shock of being pregnant I was thrilled about being a mum.' She swallowed hard. 'Sorry. I can't talk about it any more. Not right now.'

Ant had the feeling that she'd kept all the hurt inside, the same way he had. 'It's OK,' he said. 'If you decide you want to talk later, I'll be here.'

'Thank you,' she said. 'I didn't deal with it very well.'

She'd given him a pretty good clue as to why her marriage had ended. It hadn't been her fault, or her ex's. Just circumstances that had overwhelmed them both.

But maybe she'd find the strength to let out all the hurt to him, and then she could start to heal—just as she'd helped him to finally see a way forward.

On their day off, Ant made breakfast. 'Are you sure you're up to this?' he asked.

'No,' she admitted. 'None of my friends has had a baby yet, so I haven't needed to buy baby things as a present. And I never got to the shopping stage for…' She took a deep breath. 'For my baby. There wasn't time to plan a nursery, make a list of names. But it's time I made myself move on. Face what normal people do. So I'll go with you and help you choose something nice for your niece.'

'My niece,' he said. And the words didn't sting as much as he'd expected. 'I appreciate this,' he said.

'We're helping each other,' she said.

When they walked into the baby section of a big department store, she went very, very quiet for about three minutes—and then she went into sparkle mode, picking out beautiful outfits and first books and nursery accessories, full of enthusiasm and smiles.

'We don't really have these in England,' she said, picking up a flat cloth with a tiger's head peeping over the centre of one side, and knotted corners to act as paws.

'It's a *doudou plat*,' he said. 'A comfort cloth, I guess you'd call it. And that one's very cute. I'll buy it.'

'And these cot mobiles are absolutely lovely.' She stopped by one with a sun, rainbow and white fluffy clouds hanging down, and set the clockwork mechanism going; the mobile turned round to a musical box version of 'Somewhere Over the Rainbow'.

'Perfect for you, Monsieur le Nuage,' she teased.

'Actually, that's Docteur le Nuage to you,' he retorted. And then, because he couldn't help himself, he said, 'And it suits you, too, Docteur le Petit Rayon.'

'You are so bad,' she said, smiling.

But the smile didn't quite reach her eyes. Not because he'd upset her, he knew; this was fast becoming a running joke between them and she'd been the one to bring it up. She was clearly having a really hard time with this. 'Is this the sort of thing you would've bought?' he asked.

'I don't know,' she said. 'I don't usually let myself think about it.'

He took her hand. 'That was tactless of me. I apologise.'

'No need to apologise. I know I need to move on,' she said. 'But don't buy the mobile. They might already have one. Anyway, you need a panda as well as a tiger.'

'Soft toys it is.' He walked over to the display with her.

'Oh, yes!' She picked up a small plush panda and cuddled it. 'This is incredibly soft. You need this one.'

'But look, they have a white tiger,' he said, spotting one on the display stand.

'You've already got a tiger with the *doudou*. I vote for the panda.'

'Tiger,' he said implacably.

She narrowed her eyes at him and took a coin from her purse. 'Heads or tails?'

'Tails,' he said.

She tossed the coin and caught it between the back of her left hand and the palm of her right hand. 'Tails it's the tiger, heads it's the panda,' she said, before taking her right hand away. 'Oh. Tiger it is,' she said regretfully.

'Thank you. I'll get the store to wrap and deliver it for me.'

'Mind if I go and browse the craft section while you're sorting that out?'

In other words, she needed to escape from the nursery section. But she'd done well to keep there this long. 'Sure,' he said.

Once he'd bought a card and written it out, paid for his goods to be gift-wrapped and shipped and given the assistant the address for delivery, he went to find Geri in the craft section.

There seemed to be children everywhere, and she'd gone quiet again. Maybe a sunny Saturday afternoon wouldn't be the best time to take her to a park in Paris.

'I have a spontaneous suggestion for you,' he said.

'I'm listening.'

And definitely in fake-it-till-you-make-it mode, with that smile. 'It's a nice day,' he said. 'Let's get out of the city. I thought we could go to Epernay.'

'That'd be nice,' she said.

He'd make that smile a genuine one if it killed him.

'We'll take a picnic,' he said.

'With a wicker basket and a checked cloth?'

'If we take a quick diversion to the household section, yes,' he said.

She laughed. 'We can manage without a basket. But I'm curious to see what a French picnic's like.'

'What's the English version?' he asked.

'It depends. If Mum's in charge, it'll be coronation chicken and salads followed by freshly baked scones with jam and cream. If it's me or Alex, my sister, then it's sandwiches plus whatever nice things we can find in the supermarket deli.'

'In a wicker basket with a checked cloth?'

'Actually, my picnic blanket has rainbow stripes,' she said. 'But yes. And Pimm's for those who aren't driving.'

'I don't have a picnic blanket.' He'd left

the house he shared with Céline with absolutely nothing, because he hadn't wanted any reminders of the life they'd made together. 'We'd better go to the household section, I think.'

Armed with a wicker basket and a checked cloth, they headed back to Montmartre. In the street next to Antoine's apartment, they bought bread, cheese, a quiche, madeleines, and a pot of aioli to go with the tomatoes, cucumber and radishes. They bought a punnet of strawberries and a bunch of green seedless grapes as well.

'A feast fit for a queen,' he declared.

'No Pimm's?'

'I have something else in mind,' he said. 'We'll have water and coffee with the picnic.'

While she packed the picnic hamper, he made a flask of coffee and checked his phone to book a tour slot, then drove her out towards Epernay, through gently rolling countryside, with the road before them like a pale ribbon through fields of vines. There were forested hills in the distance, and little villages where the houses were built of pale stone with terracotta roofs while the churches had pyramidal lead steeples.

'This is very pretty,' she said.

'At the end of next month, when the sunflowers come out, it's even prettier,' he said. 'Provence doesn't have the monopoly on sunflowers in France, you know. Van Gogh painted some of his sunflowers at Auvers-sur-Oise, a little north of where we're heading.' He risked a glance; this time, her smile was genuine rather than overbright. 'We can explore there another day, if you like.'

'I would,' she said.

They stopped in a little village and found a picnic spot overlooking the River Marne where the water looked turquoise in the sunlight.

'Good, simple food, fresh air and good company—the perfect lunch,' she said.

Knowing that she enjoyed being with him as much as he enjoyed being with her warmed him all the way through and made him feel as if the summer was blooming with possibilities. 'I'll drink to that,' he said, and raised his mug of coffee.

'No Pimm's. Not even elderflower,' she grumbled, but she was laughing. Her hair glinted in the sunlight—she really *was* the ray of sunshine he teased her about being— and that smile was definitely genuine. He knew he'd made the right call.

'Patience,' he said. 'Good things come to those who wait.'

Once they'd finished their picnic, he drove her to Epernay. 'This,' he said as they passed the grand buildings with their wrought-iron gates, 'is the Avenue de Champagne, where all the major champagne houses have a base. Between them, they have more than a hundred kilometres of cellars under the road, and the contents are apparently worth more than the Champs-Élysées.'

She grinned. 'You looked that up.'

'Yes, because this isn't Paris or the Loire Valley.' He looked at her. 'Maybe you'd like to visit my family's vineyard at some point.'

'I'd really like that,' she said.

'Even though I know you'll end up in cahoots with my mother and my sister,' he said, 'and nag me about working too hard.'

'I might be on your side, there,' she said. 'Because we have the same job. Though I take a lunchbreak.'

'So do I,' he protested.

'A sandwich at your desk isn't the same. Learn to delegate,' she said. 'Plus having a break means you'll be fresher and more productive.'

He rolled his eyes. 'If that's what you call being on my side...'

'I am,' she said, and punched his arm lightly. 'I want you to be happy, Ant.'

'I want you to be happy, too.' All of a sudden, it felt as if the air had been sucked out round them and he felt dizzy with the possibilities. If he hadn't been driving, he would've drawn her into his arms and kissed her until she was as breathless as he felt.

'What would make you happy?' he asked.

'What would make *you* happy?' she countered.

'I asked first,' he reminded her.

What would make her happy?

What she hadn't been able to have with Mark. A relationship with someone who wanted the same things that she did. A baby. Though that was all too much to dump on Antoine. Particularly as she still didn't know if a baby was even an option. Until she tried to get pregnant, they wouldn't know how bad the damage from the Q fever had been.

'I'm happy now,' she said. 'I love my family, I love my job, and I love Paris.'

'And?' he asked.

Busted. She'd expected him to be polite and let her get away with it. Wrong. He'd give her that Parisian stare until she caved in and told him. 'A relationship,' she said. 'I think I'm ready to move on.' Just as long as she could get through this next week. The anniversary that always dragged her under the surface. 'Your turn,' she said.

He blew out a breath. 'I love my job. I'd like my family back together again, and you've helped me take the first steps in doing that.' He was silent for a while. 'And, yes, I'd like a relationship.' He paused. 'A family of my own.'

She remembered what her sister had said. Was Alex right? Should she have a mad fling? But that wasn't enough for her. She wanted something that would last. A family.

He wanted that, too. But there was the bit they hadn't talked about. The bit she couldn't handle talking about, right now: the reason for her miscarriage and the spectre of future complications. Was it fair to start something when she might not be able to deliver? It was what had held her back from dating again in England; and it stuck in her throat now, stilling her words.

She'd gone quiet on him. Maybe she, like he, was worried they were getting in too deep. Time to give her a let-out, he thought, and parked the car. 'But right now,' he said, 'I want to go on the wine tour I booked for us.'

'A wine tour? That's lovely,' she said.

'Though it might be a bit dull for you, given that your family makes wine.'

'We don't make sparkling wine,' he said. 'But I'll let Mélie tell you all the technical stuff at the vineyard. I'll quiz you afterwards. Any wrong answers mean you have to pay a forfeit.'

Oh, dear God. What on earth had possessed him to say that? He was about to apologise and backtrack when she laughed and poked him in the chest. 'If we're talking about forfeits, Monsieur le Nuage, remember that my sister is a personal trainer. And she's taught me how to do some very evil burpees.'

He'd been thinking of kisses. 'We'll discuss that later,' he said, catching her hand and feeling almost breathless at the thought of her mouth exploring his. 'I didn't have burpees in mind.'

It had been so long since he'd flirted with someone that the little exchange left him completely flustered, and Ant found it hard to pay attention to the first bit of the talk at the champagne house. But wandering round the cellars, discovering how huge the tunnels were and seeing bottles of champagne that were a couple of centuries old, was fascinating. And it felt natural to slide his arm round her shoulder, draw her close. A moment later, her arm slid round his waist. Despite the coolness of the cellars, his temperature rocketed.

After the tour, there was a chance to taste three different types of champagne.

'I'm driving,' Ant said. 'I'll take a sip of the first pour—but please have my share of the rest.'

'Thank you,' she said. 'I see what you meant now about waiting for good things. I've never done wine-tasting before, let alone tasting champagne—and this is wonderful. Pink champagne definitely beats Pimm's.'

'Good. Let me take a snap of you for your *maman*. Raise your glass in a toast.' He made sure to use his own phone for the photograph, because right then she looked really cute and he wanted to preserve the moment for himself, too.

He wasn't surprised that the rosé champagne was her favourite; and he liked the way she had the confidence to ask the sommelier questions in French, even though she needed him to translate a couple of words for her. The sommelier was charmed by her, and brought out a non-vintage bottle of rosé champagne and a sabre. 'This is the best way to open a bottle of champagne—and I shall enjoy teaching you,' he said, and proceeded to talk her through the art of sabrage.

'Am I really going to do this?' She gave Ant a worried look. 'What if I mess it up?'

'If you can anaesthetise a tiger,' he said, 'you can sabrage a bottle of champagne. You don't need brute force, you need precision—like the way you put a blade in the right place when you intubate.'

'You can anaesthetise a tiger?' the sommelier asked, looking impressed.

'We're both vets at the Zoo de Bélvèdere in Paris,' Geri explained.

'This is much, much easier—and much safer—than handling a tiger,' the sommelier said with a smile. 'Tap the blade where I show you.'

She handed her phone to Ant. 'Would you mind taking a film of this?'

'For your family? Of course,' he said.

As Ant expected, Geri executed the manoeuvre perfectly, and the sommelier gave her the cork, still embedded in the ring of the neck of the bottle.

'Bravo,' the sommelier said.

Everyone clapped, and the sommelier poured another round of champagne.

At the end of the tasting, Geri bought a couple of bottles of the rosé champagne, and Ant insisted on carrying them back to the car.

Outside the gates, she tripped, and he caught her before she fell flat on her face.

He couldn't help cradling her protectively; and in turn she wrapped her arms round him. Just as she'd held him close in the cellars.

It would be oh, so easy just to dip his head and brush his mouth against hers…

'Whoops. I'm not used to drinking in the afternoon,' she said. 'I think the champagne and the sunshine have gone to my head.'

And that made him straighten up again. He wasn't going to take advantage of her while she was tipsy. If—*when*, he thought as his heart skipped a beat—he kissed her, he wanted her to be fully in the moment, too. 'It's fine,' he said instead with a smile.

Though he kept his arm round her all the way to the car—and it wasn't only to make sure she didn't fall. He liked the way she felt in his arms. And maybe, just maybe, this could be good for both of them. He just needed to find the courage to ask her.

CHAPTER SEVEN

On Monday morning, Rico, the main keeper who looked after the cheetahs, brought up a case at the usual daybook meeting. 'I think Étoile is about to give birth,' he said.

Geri knew that in the wild cheetahs tended to hide their pregnancy until a couple of days before they gave birth, to keep the cubs safe. 'What signs have you noticed?' she asked.

'She's a bit restless,' he said. 'And her daughter from her litter last year was sniffing her belly this morning.'

'Do you think she might be lactating?' Antoine asked.

'It's possible,' Rico said. 'I'm going to rig up a birthing pen for her in the enclosure, just in case. A small pen with only one entrance, so she feels safe when she's at her most vulnerable. I'm going to put some cameras up to keep an eye on her, but I'll make sure they're high enough to avoid causing her any stress.'

'Good plan,' Antoine said. 'And will you bring her in at night this week, until we know what's going on?'

'Definitely,' Rico said. 'I'll make sure the night keeper team keeps a special eye out.'

'You mean,' Belle said drily, 'you'll find an excuse to come back and watch over her.'

Rico gave her a bashful grin. 'Maybe. But, hey, if my girl is having cubs, I want to be there. Just as you were there last year when Leylani had cubs.' Leylani was the zoo's other female Bengal tiger, who'd given birth to twin cubs the previous summer.

'And if anything happens,' Antoine said, 'you might need a vet on standby.'

'Of course, I'll call you,' Rico promised.

Geri and Antoine had almost finished dinner that evening when Antoine's mobile phone rang. He glanced at the screen.

'Everything OK? Is that Rico calling about Étoile?' Geri asked.

'No. It's Jean-Luc.'

His expression was completely unreadable. Geri decided to aim for tact. 'I'll give you some space. I'll be reading on the terrace if you need anything,' she said, heading to her room to pick up the copy of *Bonjour Tristesse* that she'd borrowed from Émilie and avoiding the dining room to give Antoine some privacy.

This would be his first contact with his brother since the day Jean-Luc had left with Céline. She really hoped that it would mend some fences between them, because she knew it had been hard for Antoine to make that first step and send a gift and card for the baby. She forced herself to concentrate on her book and made notes of unfamiliar words she needed to look up later.

Finally, Antoine came out onto the terrace, bearing two cups of chamomile tea, hers sweetened with honey. Geri suppressed the urge to ask him how his call had gone and waited for him to initiate the conversation. He was silent for a long, long time; then, finally, he looked at her. 'Thank you, Geri. Without you nudging me, I wouldn't have sent a card or a present—and the distance between us would've grown even greater.'

'It helped?' she asked.

He blew out a breath. 'It was…strange. For both of us. We were really close, and then…' He shook his head. 'It is as it is. The baby's doing well. They're all happy. Jean-Luc asked me to visit.'

'Is that what you want?'

He was silent, clearly thinking about it.

And then he nodded. 'The anger's gone. And the hurt. Now, I simply miss them.'

'Then go to see them,' she said gently. 'You've done the really hard bit, taking that first step. And it sounds as if Jean-Luc's trying to meet you halfway.'

'He said he missed me. They both did,' Antoine said. 'I admit, I can be surly and I tend to keep my distance from people. But I never used to be like that.'

He hadn't kept his distance from her at the weekend, Geri thought. He'd told her what he really wanted. That moment when she'd tripped and nearly fallen over—he'd caught her, but then he'd held her close. And she'd been near to tipping her head back, inviting him to kiss her… Particularly when he'd kept his arm around her all the way back to the car.

Then she'd fallen asleep. He was back to being professional with her when she woke, and she'd lost her nerve. 'I'm glad you're starting to patch things up,' she said. 'And if you—'

But, before she could suggest supporting him when he went to visit Céline and Jean-Luc, Antoine's phone rang again.

'It's Rico,' he said, and switched the phone

to speaker. 'Rico? You have news about Étoile?'

'I'm on my way to the zoo. Rémi—' one of the night keepers '—says she's gone into the pen, and he took a look at the video feed. There were ripples across her belly.'

'That sounds like possible contractions,' Geri said.

'I agree. I'm on my way,' Antoine said. He looked at Geri as he ended the call. 'Want to come?'

'And potentially see newborn cheetah cubs? Don't even *think* about trying to stop me,' she said with a smile.

Antoine drove them over to the zoo; the security guard let them in, and they headed over to the cheetah house.

Rico and the night keeper were both watching the video screen. The cheetah was pacing; then she lay down on her side, lifted her leg, and the first cub slithered out.

'Oh, my God,' Geri whispered. 'This is such a privilege.'

Étoile cleaned the birth sac off the cub, then lay down and let the cub wriggle its way across to start feeding.

'It's magical.' Rico was close to tears. 'My clever girl.'

An hour later, the cheetah covered the first

cub with straw, as if to hide its scent, then gave birth to her second cub; and an hour after that, she gave birth to the third.

It didn't matter that it was half-past one in the morning. Geri wouldn't have missed it for the world.

'Look at them,' she whispered. 'They're gorgeous.' All three cubs had dark markings on their face; some spots were visible on their lower bodies, but they all had a thick greyish mane. She knew it was to help camouflage them, and they wouldn't lose that part of their coat until they were about three months old.

'We'll let her bond with them without any interference,' Rico said. 'We'll do the first health checks at about ten days.'

'Vaccines at six weeks, and then we'll be able to tell the sex of the cubs,' Antoine added. 'But for now they look gorgeous.'

Geri could see his expression softening as he looked at the cubs, and it made her feel all warm and gooey. Just then, he caught her eye, and the brief smile that made the corners of his eyes crinkle was all for her. And it felt like a deeper connection, too: they were here, together, doing what they both loved.

'I know the PR team will be dying to announce the news,' Rico said, 'but I don't want Étoile spooked or crowded by visitors.'

'We don't want her to feel she has to move the cubs. Let's limit access to the cheetah house to keepers and vets only, for the next ten days—until the cubs open their eyes and Étoile's settled,' Antoine suggested. 'And maybe we can hook the cameras up to the website for a few minutes, several times a day, to let our visitors feel they still get to share the cubs.'

'At Cambridge, we'd call it cubcam,' Geri said. 'Which is short and to the point.'

'*Webcam des petits guépards,*' Rico said. 'Yeah. You're right. It's too long. Cubcam is better.'

'And you three need to get some sleep before you start in the morning,' the night keeper pointed out.

'I'm not going anywhere,' Rico said. 'I need to sort some food and water for Étoile, because she's not going to want to leave the cubs. But you two—see you tomorrow,' he said.

With a last lingering look at the cubs, who were snuggled up to their mum and fast asleep, Geri and Antoine left the zoo.

The next morning, they were in early as usual for the daybook meeting, but Rico came in looking grim. 'One of the cubs is poorly—

it's possible that Étoile rejected him while I took a couple of hours' nap in the rest room. Belle thought at first his mum had accidentally lain on the cub, because he was in a corner of the pen and wasn't moving at all, but then she saw him move his leg. We're luring Étoile away from the cubs with some meat so we can go in and check on him.'

'If he hasn't been with her and the other cubs, he'll be cold and hungry,' Antoine said. 'Let's get him into the surgery, and we'll give him a feed and warm him up; then we'll see where we go from there.'

Fortunately everything on their list that morning was routine and could be worked around the cheetah cub. Geri was in the surgery, getting the heat pads prepared and some formula mixed with a colostrum supplement before putting the bottle into a jug of hot water to warm through, and Antoine brought the cub in from the pen, tucked into his shirt to let the cub get some of his body heat.

Geri checked the cub's temperature with a thermometer gun. 'He's too cold for his temperature to register on the thermometer,' she said.

'I wondered if that might be the case.' Antoine looked grim. 'And he's floppy because he's cold. Let's give him a feed and see if we can warm him up a bit. Then we'll check him over to see if there are any problems.' He wrapped the cub in a towel with heat pads while Geri double-checked the temperature of the formula.

'OK. It's ready,' she said.

'Let's get this into you, little one,' Antoine said softly, and rubbed a couple of drops of milk onto the cub's mouth.

To their relief, the cub responded, sniffing for the teat and then sucking a few mouthfuls of milk.

Geri's heart squeezed, when she saw how gentle Antoine was with the tiny cub. Just as he'd be with a baby…

She had to swallow the lump in her throat. 'What are we going to do with you, little one?'

'Put him back in the den, once he's warm and fed. We need to give Étoile a chance to bond with the cub. If we hand-rear him, we'll have to find him a home because he won't fit into the pack here—he'll be seen as a threat and they'll kill him,' Antoine said. 'But first, we need him warmed up until his pads are the same temperature as his body, and his mouth and tongue are both pink.'

They took it in turns with Rico and Belle

to sit cradling the cub, and by the afternoon his temperature was back up and he'd taken some more milk.

'Let's get him back to his mum,' Antoine said, handing the cub back to Rico.

'I'll stay tonight,' Rico said.

'You stayed last night,' Antoine said. 'And you haven't been home yet. I'll stay tonight, and I promise I'll call if there's any change.'

'And I'll stay with you,' Geri said. 'I'm not going to settle until I know the little one's doing all right.'

That evening, Antoine and Geri made themselves comfortable in the staff room, with a monitor hooked up to the cubcam to let them see Étoile and the babies.

'Have you done many night vigils like this?' Antoine asked.

'I've done a few callouts that turned into all-nighters where we had a cow with a difficult first labour,' she said. 'And, at the zoo, we had a rota system for a couple of nights when we had a lioness we needed to keep an eye on.'

'The zoo's strange at night,' he said. 'The calls of the howler monkeys at sunset—it always makes me think of an animatronic dinosaur my grandparents took me to see when I was young.'

'I'd never thought of that before,' she said, 'but you're right.'

They kept the conversation light and un-complicated; but eventually she could feel her eyelids drooping.

'Have a nap,' Antoine said.

'Only if we set an alarm for an hour's time; then I take over watching while you have a nap,' she said.

'Two hours is probably better,' he said, and set an alarm on his phone.

Geri drifted off to sleep; when the alarm woke her, she realised that her head was pillowed on Antoine's shoulder and his arm was round her. It felt absolutely right; she allowed herself a moment to savour it. But was she too close for Antoine's comfort? Since the afternoon when he'd admitted he wanted a relationship, he'd kept her firmly in the friend zone. She sat up straight. 'Sorry for draping myself over you.'

'*De rien,*' he said. Though she couldn't tell a thing from his expression.

'How's our cub doing?' she asked.

'Étoile's let him cuddle up with the other two, which is a good sign. He hasn't fed, yet, but maybe soon,' he said.

'Let's hope,' she said. 'Now, it's your turn to sleep. I'm going to set my phone and grab a drink of water.'

When she sat down again, Antoine had drifted off to sleep. A couple of minutes later, she felt him shift next to her, and his head ended up on her shoulder. Again, it felt *right*, and she enjoyed the closeness.

In the few short weeks since she'd known him, she'd grown to like him. More than like him. She was pretty sure that he felt the same way that she did—attracted to her, but scared to trust his heart to anyone. Although she could name a dozen reasons why getting involved would be a bad idea for both of them, she still couldn't help wondering: what if they gave in to the temptation? Would it help to heal them both?

When the alarm went off, two hours later, he was awake immediately. 'Sorry for using you as a pillow.'

'*De rien,*' she said with a smile. 'Still no feed, but he's still sleeping as part of the litter.'

'That's good.' He stretched, then slid his arm round her shoulders. 'My turn for pillow duty.'

Every nerve-end zinged and her pulse rocketed. All she would have to do was turn her head slightly and reach up, slide her palm along his cheek and tip his head down so his mouth met hers…

But they were at work. This wasn't appropriate, she reminded herself. Instead, she rested her head against his shoulder, telling herself that this was what any colleague would do in the circumstances.

He woke her forty minutes later.

Bleary-eyed, she looked at him. 'What's happening?'

'You really won't want to miss this.' He gestured to the video monitor.

All three cubs were lined up, feeding from their mum.

'She's accepted him,' Geri whispered in awe.

'I think it's going to be all right, now,' he said.

It was natural to hug him in the sheer joy of the moment.

And even more natural for their cheeks to press together. For their heads to turn very, very slightly towards each other. For their lips to graze each other's. Once. Twice.

And then they were really kissing. He had one hand tangled in her hair and the other arm wrapped round her waist, and she was holding him tightly. Little sparkles of pleasure ran through her as his mouth moved over hers, nipping gently and urging her to open her mouth and let him deepen the kiss.

Desire surged through her, making her feel dizzy. She was glad they were sitting down, because she was pretty sure her knees had both turned to jelly.

When he broke the kiss, they were both shaking.

'I'm sorry—I shouldn't have done that,' he said, taking his hand out of her hair and dropping his arm from her waist.

But there was yearning in his eyes, not distaste.

'I think it was both of us,' she said. If Antoine was backing off, she had nothing to lose. She took her courage in both hands. 'We could say it was the heat of the moment, and blame it on the joy of seeing the cub accepted by his mum. But I think it's been coming for a while.'

He was silent for such a long time that she started to think she'd got it very badly wrong, and horror seeped through her. Oh, God. Work was going to be awkward in the extreme, now—and she'd have to move out. No way could she stay with him after what she'd said.

'You're right,' he said. 'It's been there for

a while for me, too. But I…' He dragged in a breath. 'You know my situation. I think yours might be a little complicated, too.'

It was. And she hadn't told him everything about the baby. She'd been too focused on trying to block out the fact that the anniversary was ticking round: a day that always felt like lead and where it was as much as she could do to put one foot in front of another. 'Yes,' she whispered.

He stroked her cheek, his dark eyes full of emotion. 'Then we should be sensible.'

She knew he was right, but at the same time her shoulders sagged with disappointment. 'I'll make us some coffee,' she said, wanting to put a little physical distance between them while she got her head in the right place.

'Thanks. I'll take some film of this for Rico and Belle.'

If she thought about it logically, she definitely shouldn't get involved with him. They lived in different countries. What would happen at the end of her secondment? Would he be prepared to give up everything for her and live in England? Or would he expect her to give up everything and settle in France?

She'd been here before, in a situation where there wasn't a workable compromise. Her marriage had broken up as a result. It would be crazy to get involved with a man who was still coming to terms with being dumped on his wedding day. Maybe instead of helping to heal each other, they'd only make things worse.

They needed to be strictly colleagues and friends. Even though part of her wanted more, she was going to be sensible. And she was glad she'd made that decision, half an hour later, when Rico walked in to check on the cub's progress. Supposing he'd walked in when she and Antoine had been kissing?

'I know it's barely dawn,' Rico said, 'but I couldn't sleep.'

'Worrying about the cub?' Geri asked.

'Yeah.' He looked up at the monitor. 'They're all asleep. Together. That's a good sign.'

'Better than that,' Antoine said. He flicked into the photos app and handed his phone to Rico. 'I took this earlier because I thought you'd want to see it.'

Rico was silent as he watched the film of all three cubs lined up and feeding, and although he was smiling broadly by the end his eyes were full of tears. 'Our cub's got a fighting chance, now.'

'It looks like it,' Geri said.

For a moment, her eyes met Antoine's. She could see he was glad about the cub; but was that a hint of regret she could see in his face, or was that wishful thinking?

By the end of the week, Étoile had accepted the cub completely, and the cubcam had become the most popular page on the zoo's website.

Ant had arranged to visit Jean-Luc, Céline and baby Maya at their home in Chartres on Saturday.

'I know this might be a big ask,' he said to Geri, 'but you're welcome to come with me. You don't have to meet Jean-Luc or Céline or see the baby. Just have a wander round Chartres, because it's pretty there and I think you'd like it.'

She stared at him, saying nothing.

Of course it had been stupid to ask her.

But then he realised there was a tear running down her face. And another. And another. She was crying silently, and to him it looked as if her heart was breaking.

'What's wrong?' he asked.

She scrubbed at her face. 'Nothing.'

It didn't look like nothing to him.

'This happens once in a while,' she said.

And that was even more worrying.

How did he get her to open up to him? She'd been a bit super-smiley with him since the night they'd ended up kissing and he'd called a halt; and she'd kept him at a slight distance, too.

He busied himself making her a milky cup of tea, exactly the way she liked it.

'The English solution to everything?' she asked wryly.

'It's obvious something's wrong, Geri. Talk to me.'

'It's not important. And you're supposed to be leaving for Chartres, or you'll be late.'

She had a point. Seeing her in tears had made him forget everything else. 'One moment,' he said.

He quickly texted Jean-Luc.

Something's come up and I need to reschedule. Apologies for late notice. Will call later today. NOT cutting you off.

The reply came back moments later.

D'accord.

'All sorted,' he said.

'But you—' she began.

'But nothing,' he said. 'Take a sip of tea,

then take a deep breath—and tell me what's wrong. I'm not going to judge, just listen.'

She shivered, and took a sip of tea. And then she paused for such a long time that he thought she wasn't going to tell him a thing. But, finally, she started speaking. 'Today's the anniversary.' She swallowed hard. 'Of the day my life turned upside down.'

'The day you lost the baby?' he guessed.

She squeezed her eyes shut. 'My life started turning upside down a few weeks before then, I guess, though I didn't know it at the time. I worked in a practice dealing with farm animals. One of our clients had problems with a ewe, and I was on call, so I went to help.'

A ewe.

A few weeks ago from now would have meant late April.

Lambing season.

Ant had a nasty feeling he knew exactly what Geri was about to tell him. If he'd been the senior vet at her practice, he would never have allowed her to go on that call.

'I didn't have a clue I might've been pregnant, and Mark and I weren't even trying for a baby, or I would've asked someone else to take the call for me,' she said, almost as if she'd read his mind.

What had she contracted? Campylobacte-riosis? Chlamydia? There were a number of zoonotic diseases in sheep that could cause women to lose a baby, Ant knew, which was why pregnant women were advised to avoid sheep at lambing time.

'If I'd had any idea there was *coxiella bur-netii* on the farm…' She shook her head. 'But the flock had no symptoms of Q fever what-soever. As far as I was concerned, I was sim-ply helping a ewe with a difficult birth—a lamb that was stuck. We had a good outcome, and the mum and the lamb were both doing well. I had a mug of tea with the farmer; we discussed how the new lambs were doing, and whether he was expecting difficulties with any of the other ewes. There was no reason to think that anything else might go wrong.'

Ant remembered from his training that Q fever spread by contact of abrasions with bodily fluids, or by inhalation of spores. He was pretty sure that Geri would've used gloves if she'd had a cut on her hands; she must've caught the infection through simply breathing normally while she was treating the ewe. A symptomless flock meant that nobody could have known there was a potential prob-lem and taken precautions to avoid it.

Her face was filled with anguish, and he couldn't stay on the other side of the table from her any longer. She needed to get the words out, but he was also sure that she needed comfort—and that was something he could do for her. He pushed his chair back, walked round to her, scooped her up and sat in her chair, settling her on his lap and holding her close. 'I'm here,' he said quietly. 'I'm listening. None of this was your fault, Geri.'

'It feels like it,' she whispered.

'It absolutely was *not* your fault,' he repeated. 'Keep talking. Remember, you told me how sometimes talking about things can take the pressure out of your head. You were right. Talk to me and let it out, instead of letting it squash you.'

She slid her arms round him, and he was glad that she was clearly taking comfort from his nearness.

'Two weeks after I delivered the lamb, I went down with what I thought was some kind of spring flu. I was bone-deep tired, I had a banging headache and my muscles ached all over. I couldn't shift it. The covid test was negative; my GP—my family doctor—took bloods to see what was going on.' She closed her eyes for a moment, clearly haunted by the memory. 'The results came back positive for *coxiella burnetii.* She said I had Q fever, and asked me if I was pregnant because the usual treatments are dangerous for unborn babies. I was about to say no—but then I realised I hadn't had a period for a while.' She grimaced. 'Which isn't me being scatty. My periods have always been all over the place.'

'You're the least scatty person I know,' Antoine said, stroking her hair.

'Thank you.' Her breath shuddered. 'The doctor asked me to do a pregnancy test before she could prescribe anything. I was utterly shocked to see that second blue line come up. And I was utterly horrified to realise I'd put a baby at risk.'

'You couldn't have known about the *coxiella burnetii* or the baby,' he said, holding her close. 'It's not your fault. It's not anybody's fault. It was simply bad luck.'

'The doctor started treating me with cotrimoxazole,' she said. 'But it was too late. I lost the baby two weeks later, at what we think must've been about ten weeks.' She closed her eyes. 'Three years ago today.'

'I'm so very sorry,' he said, holding her more tightly.

'It's like being wrapped in lead,' she said. 'Most of the time I'm OK. But this day of the year—it just flattens me. It feels full of shadows. Whatever I do.'

'Of course it does. It doesn't matter that it was early on, or that you hadn't planned the baby; it's still a loss and of course it's going to hurt.'

She leaned her forehead against his. 'Thank you. For understanding.'

'I'm here.' He stroked her hair.

'And then afterwards, it made me realise that actually, I *did* want children. But Mark still didn't. He'd had a fairly miserable childhood, and his parents had an acrimonious divorce. Even though he'd met my family and they were proof that family life didn't always have to be difficult, he still didn't want children.' She grimaced. 'He liked things ordered and pristine. We even had white furniture and white carpets—which absolutely aren't sensible to have with small children or pets. We talked about it, but he was shocked by the idea that we might've been parents. And then it got worse. He said he didn't have a role model, growing up, and he couldn't see himself as a dad. Ever.' She sighed. 'We kept going round and round in circles. I think losing the baby changed us both; it made him more adamant that he didn't want children. But I did, and there wasn't a real compromise.

You can't have half a baby. One of us had to give up our dream, and it wouldn't be fair on the other. Eventually we agreed it would be better to end our marriage, and we split the house and everything down the middle. Mark was fair about it—he wasn't selfish.'

Not selfish? Ant wasn't quite as sure about that. Financially, her ex had been fair; emotionally, could he have done more? 'Though he wasn't prepared to raise children with you?'

'Mark was—*is*—a good man,' Geri said. 'We loved each other, but in the end that turned out to be not quite enough. He didn't want to hurt me, but how could he force himself to do something to please me that would've made him hugely unhappy? And in the long run it would've hurt us more—if we'd had a child and *then* split up, it would've hurt our child, too. He'd been collateral damage himself, and he didn't want to be the one inflicting that on a child of his own.' She spread her hands. 'We talked and talked and talked about it, and in the end this seemed the fairest solution for both of us.'

'I'm sorry,' he said, holding her close.

'He's found someone else now and they see things the same way. Neither of them want children, and they're happy together.'

She gave him a watery smile. 'And I'm truly glad for him. I didn't want to see him lonely and miserable.'

Of course she didn't. Geri was lovely—and she *cared*. It was one of the things he liked so much about her.

'I didn't want to go back to working with farm animals—not when working with the sheep had made everything go wrong for me. That was when I decided to switch specialties,' she said. 'I did my Masters in London, living with my parents while I studied, and then I got the job at Cambridge.'

'And you're happy in your new role?'

'I am,' she said. 'I really do love my job.'

'But what about you?' he asked. 'You said you wanted a relationship.'

She nodded. 'But, before I get properly involved with someone else, I want to make sure that my future partner and I really do want the same things.'

She'd met *him*. Could he be her future partner? Did she want the same things that he did?

'And you still want children?' he asked carefully.

'I do—but it's going to be a bit more complicated now,' she said. 'Because of the Q fever, it's possible that I'm at a higher risk of losing my next baby. And it's also possible that the Q fever might be reactivated during pregnancy. I know the doctors will give me more blood tests to check, and they'll keep a really close eye on me, but…' She grimaced. 'If I ever get pregnant again, I'm going to be worrying all the way through the pregnancy.'

'Which is only natural, considering what happened to you,' he said.

'The doctors gave me medication for a year after I lost the baby. I know at least I'm not at risk of developing endocarditis,' she said. 'But they told me it might be tricky getting pregnant and staying pregnant.'

'That's understandable, given what's happened,' he said.

'I hope my future partner will think that way,' she said.

He did; but now wasn't the right time to push her to consider him as a future partner, Ant thought. Particularly as he knew he was as damaged as she was. But maybe, just maybe, he could help her through today. And then they could see where this took them.

'I'm sorry that happened to you,' he said. 'Losing a baby and then losing your marriage. That's hard.'

She nodded.

'You told me you always looked for the sunshine—how, when this happened to you?'

'I was really low for a couple of months after I lost the baby. My sister was brilliant; she bossed me about and made me do her classes. And eventually I realised I could either stay miserable, and people around me would worry about me all the time and it'd be a vicious circle; or I could try and look for the bright stuff in life. That's how I learned to fake it—to stop everyone worrying about me.' She shrugged.

Except suppressing her feelings hadn't helped her move on. It had kept her stuck. He kept his arms wrapped round her, and gradually her tears dried.

'Thank you for listening,' she said.

'Any time. And I'm sorry this happened to you, Geri. You lost more than I did.'

'No. I think we both lost what we wanted,' she said, 'and it wasn't either of our faults.'

'Maybe,' he said, 'we need to spend a while in a green space. Somewhere quiet where you won't have to face families with children. Go and splash your face with water, give me ten minutes, and I'll take you somewhere.'

Geri was grateful that Antoine had given her some space. Splashing her face with water made her feel better; by the time she heard the front door close, she felt a bit more in control.

She headed back up to the kitchen to join him, and blinked in surprise when she saw he was holding a bunch of white roses and a pair of scissors.

'The florist didn't sell dried petals,' he said, 'but I thought maybe we could drop fresh ones into a stream in remembrance of your baby.'

'That's…' The tears welled up, clogging her throat; she had to swallow hard before she could speak again. 'That's really thoughtful.'

'It's what I do on my grandmother's anniversary,' he said. 'But the place where I normally go in Paris will be full of children, and it'll be hard for you. We'll go out of the city.'

'Thank you,' she said. 'Though I feel guilty, because you were supposed to be seeing Céline and Jean-Luc and mending some bridges.'

'It's fine. And this is just as important,' he said.

She helped him cut the petals from the roses and fold them into a paper bag; then they drove north of Paris, out towards the Forest of Compiègne, and he parked the car in a pretty village. They walked past a row of cottages with pale stone walls, terracotta roofs and painted wooden shutters at the windows; climbing roses covered the trellises around the doors, and a few buds were starting to peep out. It felt almost as if they were walking back through centuries, and at any minute a carriage and horses would come down the cobbled street.

At the end of the street there was a fortified gate; a stone arch stretched between two towers with conical tiled roofs. Geri half expected it to lead to a castle, but it turned out to be a church.

'It's what's left of an old Benedictine abbey,' Ant said.

They stopped in the middle of a small stone bridge that crossed the stream, where he gave her the bag of rose petals. She scattered a handful, then offered the bag to him.

'Sleep peacefully, little one,' he said softly as he scattered the petals.

It was as if he knew the words in her heart, and she felt lighter—as if the weight of misery that normally shrouded her on this day was finally starting to dissolve.

When they finished scattering the petals and left the bridge, he took her hand; she knew this was his way of letting her know without words that he was there if she needed to lean on him, and she really appreciated it.

They walked in a comfortable silence back to the car, not needing to speak.

At the car, she squeezed his hand. 'Thank you, Antoine. For understanding. For caring. It means a lot.'

'Any time,' he said, and the warmth in his eyes made her feel as if there was brightness left in the world.

CHAPTER EIGHT

THE NEXT DAY, Geri felt as if the huge weight of grief had slid from her shoulders and she could breathe again.

'I'm sorry for sobbing all over you yesterday,' she said to Antoine over breakfast.

'It's fine,' he said. 'I understand.'

'Thank you. It's that one day in the year when it just overwhelms me,' she said. 'The day afterwards, I can cope again. But you did a lot to help. I appreciate it.'

'You're welcome,' he said. 'I've got a half-day today. Maybe we can do a bit of exploring, this afternoon—and go dancing by the Seine, this evening. Tick another thing off your list.'

'I'd really like that,' she said.

After dinner, they headed down to the Jardin de Tino Rosso, a pretty park on the left bank of the Seine. It was filled with flowers and modern sculpture, but best of all for Geri was the series of little amphitheatres by the edge of the river. There were people sitting on the curved stone steps to watch the dancers in the centre—and it seemed to be open to everyone. Some wore proper dancing shoes, some wore trainers, and others still danced in bare feet.

'You wanted to dance the tango in Paris,' Antoine said with a smile. *'Voici.'*

Geri eyed the dancers, who all seemed to know exactly what they were doing. 'I've never actually danced the tango,' she said.

'I learned here as a student,' he said. 'It was fun.'

'Maybe I should sit and watch,' she said.

'It's an open dance thing. If you sit down, someone will ask you to dance,' he said. 'You might as well dance with me.' He smiled. 'Hey. If you can anaesthetise a tiger…'

'Then I can take the cork off a champagne bottle with a sabre, and I can dance the tango,' she said.

'That's *mon petit rayon.*' The warmth in his eyes sent heat sizzling through her veins. 'Now, your sister teaches aerobics. I'm guessing you know how to follow a routine?'

'I do,' she confirmed.

He drew her over to a quieter spot. 'Let's run through the basics. Remember you'll be alternating your feet. Stand facing me, feet together,' he said. 'Take one step back with your left foot, then one to the side with your right.' He nodded in approval as she followed his instructions. 'Two steps back—left and right—then cross your left foot in front of your right.' He smiled. 'Last bit: right foot back, left foot left, close with your right, and you're ready to start again.'

'Got it,' she said.

'Good. Now do it again, and this time you'll be more or less mirroring me,' he said. Once they'd run through the sequence three or four times, he said, 'Now let's try it in hold. Put your right hand up, and hold my left.' He smiled. 'That's fine. Your left arm goes round my shoulders, and your hand goes just below my neck.'

When she'd followed his instructions, he slid his right arm round her shoulders, pulling her close to him.

'Follow my lead. We'll do the basic step,' he said.

It felt very different, when he was up close and personal. She'd never realised how broad his shoulders were, how defined his muscles were. Not only his back: his legs, too. She could feel her breath growing shallower and her pulse speeding up as they danced.

'Ready to add a bit?' he asked.

'Uh-huh,' she said, not trusting herself to use proper words. Dancing with him was definitely scrambling her brain.

He taught her how to swivel her hips, and it made her catch her breath.

She'd had no idea that the tango was *this* sensual.

'Let's try it down with everyone else,' he said. 'Follow my lead. I've got you; you won't fall.'

She had no idea how they got down to the main dance floor; all she was aware of was the sound of the music, the heat of the late spring evening, the scent of the blossom and the feel of his body close to hers.

Even though she knew there was a crowd of people in the little amphitheatre, it felt as if it was only the two of them, the music and the reflection of the streetlights shimmering on the river.

He'd dipped his head far enough to rest his cheek next to hers. Every time they turned a corner, his leg slid between hers and he held her more tightly before releasing her again. Every swivel of their hips stoked her desire higher and higher. If he didn't kiss her, and soon, she was convinced that she was going to spontaneously combust.

She tilted her face slightly, so her lips brushed the corner of his mouth; and she felt the immediate tension in his body.

'Geri, if you do that again,' he whispered, 'I can't be responsible for what happens next.'

It sounded like a challenge.

How could she resist?

She kissed him again; and this time he kissed her back, his mouth hot and sensual beneath the stars.

It wasn't enough.

Not anywhere near enough.

'Let's go home,' she whispered. 'Dance with me in your roof garden.'

'*D'accord,*' he said, his voice sounding as shaken as she felt.

He held her hand all the way on the Métro. Kissed her under every streetlight between the station and the row of houses where he lived. Kissed her in the lift up to his apartment.

'Hold that thought,' he said as they reached his front door. Once he'd unlocked it, he scooped her into his arms and carried her up the stairs and through to the kitchen. Then he let her slide down until her feet were touching the floor, before kissing her again.

'You wanted to dance,' he said, and opened the door to the roof garden. 'I don't think we have room to tango.' He found some sweet, slow music on his phone, then drew her into his arms and danced with her cheek to cheek.

The tango had felt like dancing through fire. This felt like dancing through an orchard full of blossom, with the petals gently dropping over them. And this time, when he kissed her, it was sweet and slow and made her ache.

'Antoine,' she whispered. 'I want you.'

'I want you, too, *mon petit rayon*,' he whispered back.

'Take me to bed.'

His dark gaze held hers. 'You're sure?'

She nodded. 'I've wanted you since the day we met.'

'It's the same for me,' he said. 'But—'

'No buts. We'll think about things tomorrow,' she said. 'Tonight—let's just *be*.'

He brushed his mouth against hers, sensitising every nerve-end, and she shivered. 'Ant. *Now*.'

He scooped her up, carried her back into the apartment, and then down the stairs to his bedroom.

The next morning, the alarm shrilled on Antoine's phone.

Geri woke, warm and comfortable in Antoine's arms—and then the previous night flooded back into her head.

Oh, help.

What did they do now?

They'd been carried away by the music and the dancing, and they'd both wanted each other. It had been a moment out of time. One she was glad they'd shared; but now it was Monday morning. Time to go back out of their bubble and into their normal lives.

And all of a sudden she felt ridiculously shy.

He switched off the alarm. 'Good morning.'

His voice sounded carefully neutral. Did he regret last night?

And where did they go from here?

She still felt ridiculously shy, but she wasn't a coward. She'd face this. She took a deep breath and looked him in the eye. 'Good morning.'

It wasn't only his voice that was carefully neutral; his expression was, too.

Sink or swim, she thought. 'What happens now?'

'That depends.'

Two could play at equanimity. 'On what?' she asked coolly.

'Touché,' he said. 'Last night—I have no regrets.'

Relief flooded through her. Maybe they could find a way through this that wasn't awkward. 'Me, neither.'

'Good.' He kissed the tip of her nose. 'But I'm not ready to share that with anyone else, yet. Not until we both know what we want. Perhaps at work we can let everyone think we're just friends?'

'Is that what we are?'

'I don't know,' he said. 'There are all kinds of reasons why we should be just friends. You're here for six months. We live in different countries. We both have scars across our hearts. The sensible thing would be for us to be just friends.'

'There's a "but" in your voice,' she said.

He nodded. 'I like you, *mon petit rayon*.' He paused. 'More than like.'

Her pulse kicked up a notch. 'I wasn't expecting this. I wasn't looking for another relationship.'

'But?'

She smiled. 'I like you, too. A lot. More than like. And I want to be with you, see where things go.'

'Then let's keep this between us, for now.' He stole a kiss. 'Though, this very minute, we need to get a move on or we'll be late for work.'

'And that,' she said, 'might let the cat out of the bag.' She kissed him back. 'First one to the kitchen puts the kettle on.'

'*D'accord.*' His eyes glittered. 'And, much as I'd like to scoop you up and carry you to my shower, I think you'd better use your own bathroom.'

'About the shower? Maybe we can do that tonight,' she said, and was gratified to see colour bloom across his cheeks. It was enough to remove the last vestiges of her shyness; she climbed out of his bed, scooped up her clothes and sashayed to the door, enjoying his sharp intake of breath.

In the kitchen, they had a perfectly civil breakfast of coffee and *tartine*.

But then Antoine kissed her by the front door, enough to make her knees weak.

'Hold that thought,' he said. 'Now we go into colleague mode.'

'Colleague, flatmate and friend,' she corrected.

Even so, he held her hand all the way to the Métro station, and halfway to the zoo. But then they strolled into work as if it was a perfectly normal Monday morning. Geri liked that Antoine put professionalism first and concentrated on the animals, and she was even more thrilled at the daybook meeting when he and Pierre agreed to tempt Zhen with some treats in the hope that they could do an ultrasound.

'We'll definitely know if she's pregnant?' Geri asked.

'Hopefully,' Antoine said.

Once they'd done the rounds and sorted out the morning's problems, it was time to give Zhen an ultrasound. There was an inspection hatch on the bars of her enclosure, similar to the one Antoine had used when taking bloods from Bianca's tail, and Pierre was carrying a bucket of sweet potato cubes.

'Do you want to feed our girl?' Pierre asked.

'I do—but I also want to see the ultrasound,' she said.

'Feed our girl while Ant feels her tummy,' Pierre said, 'and then when he does the ultrasound you can take a film of the screen for the zoo.'

'All right,' she said.

Zhen came into the enclosure and lay down in front of the bars of the training chute on her right side, facing them.

'I assume you do the same sort of training as they do with the tigers?' Geri asked.

'We do,' Pierre confirmed. 'Zhen and Bohai are both happy to put their paw out and grasp a bar to let us do a blood draw. We use a tennis ball on a pole as our target, and reward them with sweet potato or honey water in a squeezy tube.'

He fed Zhen a cube of sweet potato. 'Good girl,' he said. 'Paw up.'

Zhen put her left paw on the bar, and received another treat and more praise.

'Leg out,' he said, and the panda stretched out to bare her tummy.

Geri took over, soothing the panda and feeding her more potato as Antoine undid the inspection hatch. 'I can't believe how gentle she is,' she said. 'This is like giving treats to a dog or cat.'

'We all enjoy training,' Pierre said.

Antoine felt the panda's abdomen, as Pierre gave Zhen another cube and praised her.

'Time to film?' Geri asked.

'Yes,' Antoine said, and squeezed gel onto the transceiver head. 'We've warmed the gel so it isn't a shock to her,' he said.

Pierre kept soothing the panda and feeding her cubes of sweet potato while Antoine pressed the transceiver against her stomach.

'Someone's full of bamboo,' he remarked. 'Don't hold your breath, because we're looking for something the size of a marble. It's only the last two weeks of pregnancy where we get a decent view of a foetus.'

Geri held her breath as she filmed him doing the ultrasound, then switched view to the portable screen.

Would it show the amniotic sac—or was it a pseudopregnancy?

Ant moved the head of the transceiver. 'Well, now. I think we might have a sight of foetal tissue.'

The triangular image showed the denser muscles and tissues, and then the wavy dark space of Zhen's uterus, and finally the tiny white shape Antoine had mentioned earlier.

'And that's our panda foetus?' she asked.

'Probably,' Antoine said. 'We can cautiously say, as long as she doesn't resorb the foetus, with luck she'll have a cub next month.'

'I feel almost as proud as when I saw my son's ultrasound,' Pierre said feelingly. 'You clever girl, Zhen. You clever, clever girl.'

Geri stopped filming and took over feeding the sweet potato to Zhen while Pierre looked at the screen.

The keeper wiped his eyes. 'Look at me, crying like a baby.'

'I can hardly believe this,' Geri said. 'Today's a perfect day.'

Antoine stroked the panda's abdomen and took the transceiver away. 'Good girl,' he said. 'You were very patient with us.'

Pierre gave Zhen a couple more treats. 'Well done, sweetheart,' he said. 'Now go and have your bamboo.'

The panda grunted as Antoine closed the inspection hatch, and then stood up and ambled away.

That evening, Ant and Geri caught the Métro back to Montmartre. He took her hand as they left the station, and it felt so right.

'Want to go exploring, or have a quiet night in?' he asked.

'I think we'd have to toss a coin for that one,' she said with a smile. 'Either way, I'm going to talk your ears off about pandas. I've been reading up.'

He couldn't resist her enthusiasm and the way her eyes sparkled. 'Early dinner,' he said, 'then the terrace and a glass of wine.'

'Perfect,' she said. 'Did you know that a panda cub can't regulate its body temperature? That's why the mum will keep the cub tucked under her chin or her arm for the first few weeks, and breathe on it to keep its environment warm and humid.'

He did know, actually, because he'd worked in zoo medicine for a few more years than she had, but he wasn't going to stifle that enthusiasm. 'Baby pandas are hairless and blind,' he said. 'They need that warmth and humidity.'

'I really hope Zhen has that cub,' she said. 'It's incredibly exciting.' She paused. 'Today couldn't get any more perfect.'

'That sounds like a challenge,' Ant said. 'And one I fully intend to meet.'

Her eyes widened. 'I like the sound of that...'

After dinner, they strolled through the streets holding hands; he kissed her at every street corner on the way back to his apartment.

On the roof garden, he scooped Geri onto his lap and held her close. 'I've wanted to do this all day.'

'Me, too.' She stroked his face. 'I like being with you.'

'I like being with you, too. You make the world feel full of sunshine.'

'Careful. You're starting to sound like a poet,' she warned teasingly. 'Oh, wait—isn't French poetry melancholy?'

'A lot of it is,' he said. 'But some aren't.

There's the Rostand poem about a kiss being the pink dot you put on the I of the verb "to love".'

'That sounds fabulous,' she said. 'Do you know the full thing?'

'I'm a scientist,' he said. 'I didn't really learn much poetry. Hold on, and I'll find it.' He took his phone from the table and checked the internet. 'Here.'

She scanned it swiftly, then tried translating it.

'That's a good attempt,' he said, rewarding her with a kiss.

'Read it to me in the original,' she said. 'You have a beautiful voice.'

Nobody had ever said that to him before. Nobody had ever asked him to read poetry to them before. And he'd pretty much forgotten most of his literature lessons from school. But he smiled and read it to her.

'That's lovely,' she said.

'It's actually from *Cyrano de Bergerac*,' he said. 'The scene where Cyrano wins a kiss for Christian from Roxane. The film won Depardieu an award nomination.' He found the clip on the internet.

She watched it, her pupils growing darker. 'He should've won the award for that,' she said. 'But I like your version better. The words won a kiss, did they?'

'*Un bisou,*' he confirmed.

'Then that,' she said, 'should be your reward, too.'

The kiss was slow, long, and sent his pulse hammering. By the time she broke the kiss, he couldn't think straight. All he could think of was how much he wanted to kiss her again, make love to her, make her see stars.

And he only realised he'd said the words out loud when she whispered, 'Do it.'

What could he do but carry her to bed?

CHAPTER NINE

IT WAS ALMOST a perfect week, Ant thought.
He loved his work at the zoo; and he loved
spending time outside work with Geri, exploring the hidden corners of his city and
making love with her. He couldn't remember
the last time he'd been this happy.

When they both had a day off on Thursday, he took her to Versailles. It had been a
while since he'd visited, and he'd forgotten
how big the building was.

'This is breathtaking,' Geri said as they
walked into the Hall of Mirrors. 'Those huge
arched windows reflected in those enormous
mirrors, and the chandeliers—all that light!
It must've seemed even more stunning when
it was built.'

'Nearly three hundred and fifty years ago,'
he said. 'Louis XIV was determined to prove
that the French could make mirrors as well
as Venice.'

She loved the lightness of the Queen's bed-chamber, too, with the exact replicas of the original fabric.

But her favourite bit was the Grand Trianon, with its pink marble columns, chequered floors and stunning gardens. Ant liked it, too, because he got to hold her hand all the way through their visit, and to kiss her in a quiet arbour of roses.

It was another day out of time, where he felt they got closer still; but Friday was more worrying.

Matthieu, head of the primate section, looked grim. 'It's Shabani.' Shabani was the silverback—the leader of their small troop of gorillas. 'He's not been eating much, this week.'

Given that gorillas spent half their day eating, that was a bad sign. 'Is there any physical reason why he's not eating?'

'He's not been touching his favourite browse—' fresh tree trimmings '—and I wonder if he has a tooth causing pain,' Matthieu said.

Ant nodded. 'We're going to need to sedate him, to take a proper look at him.'

'Are the gorillas trained in the same way as the tigers?' Geri asked.

'No. We'll need to use a dart,' Ant said.

'One of the vet team will do it, Matthieu; we don't want to risk damaging any of the keepers' relationships with him.'

'I was hoping you'd say that. I've kept him apart from the others,' Matthieu said, 'and no food or water since last night.'

'We'll put him top of the list,' Ant said. 'Geri—airway or sedation?'

'Airway,' she said. 'And I'll do the darting. He doesn't know me, and I don't want him associating it with you in case you need to do treatment while he's conscious.'

'Thank you,' Ant said.

Shabani was in one of the indoor enclosures. Geri darted him, but Shabani pulled the dart out immediately.

'It needs to be in for a couple of seconds to get enough anaesthetic into his system,' Ant said. 'But we don't want too much, either.'

'Not on top of what he already might have had,' Geri said. 'Let's use a half dose with the second dart.'

This time, it worked. As soon as he was unconscious, a team of four keepers moved him onto his back, and Geri intubated him to keep him breathing.

Ant assessed Shabani's mouth. 'I can't see anything,' he said. 'We need an X-ray.'

He X-rayed the gorilla's jaw, but all thirty-two teeth were fine.

Gently, he explored the gorilla's face. 'There's a lump here, under his jaw,' he said.

Matthieu dragged in a breath. 'Are you thinking cancer?'

'We'd need the lab to tell us that,' Ant said. 'At the moment, it feels like soft tissue. I'm going to remove it, and we'll get it tested.'

He sterilised the area, and made only a small hole, meaning that Shabani would be less likely to pick at the stitches afterwards. He excised the lump and put it into a sample container for the lab team, then concentrated on suturing the wound.

The whole procedure took almost an hour.

'OK. We're going to reverse the anaesthetic now,' he said.

Geri removed the tube, Ant gave the injection, and they stayed outside the enclosure to monitor the gorilla.

'I think his airway might be blocked,' Ant said. 'I'll go in.'

He cleared Shabani's mouth; the gorilla growled, and Ant backed out of the enclosure.

Shabani growled again, and Matthieu gave a smothered sob.

Geri clearly noticed, because she put her

arm round his shoulders. 'It's going to be all right,' she said.

'It's just seeing him lying there, helpless… I've known him since he was a baby,' Matthieu said. 'I cuddled him when he was tiny.'

'We needed to check him out to find out what was going on, and Ant couldn't have removed that lump without anaesthetic,' Geri said. 'He's coming round, the same way as a human when they mumble a bit and it doesn't mean anything. We're here to keep an eye on him.'

She really was lovely, Ant thought. Empathetic, instinctively knowing when someone needed kindness and saying the right words to make them feel better.

After half an hour, Shabani was conscious but still a little drowsy.

'I'll keep an eye on him,' Matthieu said.

'It's nearly lunchtime,' Geri said. 'I'll get you a coffee and something to eat.'

'I'm not sure I could eat anything,' Matthieu admitted. 'I'm too worried. I'd rather stay with Shabani.'

'I'll keep you company,' Ant said.

'We both will,' Geri said. 'I'll get the equipment back to the surgery, take the lump to the lab, and bring you both some lunch.'

Matthieu gave them a watery smile. 'Sorry. But my gorillas…they're like part of the family.'

'Of course they are,' Geri said. 'I used to work with farm animals—and every single cow, sheep and pig had a name. The farmers could tell them all apart, even those who looked identical to me. They all had characters. Just because the animals here aren't domestic, it doesn't mean you don't get close to them.'

By the next morning, Shabani had his appetite back and had been reunited with his brothers; and by the middle of the week the lab came back with the good news that it wasn't anything sinister, merely an infected salivary gland.

The following Saturday, Antoine asked Geri to go to Chartres with him.

'If it's too soon for you to be around a baby, I understand,' he said. 'I don't want to reopen your scars.'

'It's not my dark day of the year. I can cope,' she said. 'But are you sure Jean-Luc and Céline won't mind me being there?'

'Jean-Luc asked me to invite you.'

Antoine had mentioned her to his brother? That felt like a huge step. 'All right,' she said.

'Provided I can take flowers and something for the baby.'

'And I'll take champagne,' he said.

Antoine was quiet on the drive, and Geri put her hand briefly over his on the steering wheel and pressed lightly. 'Are you sure you're up to this?'

'Once we're over the first awkward moments,' he said, 'I think it'll be fine. The anticipation's the worst thing.' He paused. 'Jean-Luc and I—we've been texting quite a bit, since I got back in touch. Little things, nothing deep. But it feels as if I'm getting my brother back.'

'I'm glad,' she said.

Finally, they reached Chartres and he parked on the drive; carrying the flowers, champagne and the fabric book of zoo animals Geri hadn't been able to resist, they waited on the doorstep.

Jean-Luc answered the door. For a second, everyone was frozen; and then Jean-Luc gave Antoine the biggest hug. 'My little brother,' he said, his voice thick with emotion. 'I'm so glad to see you.'

Geri was surprised by how similar they looked. The only real difference between them was in the shadows under Jean-Luc's eyes, which could all be down to the new baby. Still with his arm round Antoine's shoulders, Jean-Luc turned to her. 'You must be Geri. *Enchanté*.' He shook her hand.

'Pleased to meet you,' Geri said. '*Merci de m'avoir invitée.*'

'Come in,' Jean-Luc said, standing aside to usher them in.

Céline was walking up the hallway, carrying the baby. She looked nervous, but glanced at Jean-Luc, who gave the tiniest nod.

'Welcome,' she said.

Antoine went very still, and then he smiled. 'She's beautiful, Céline. I can see both of you in her.'

'Ant. I'm…' She blew out a breath, clearly searching for the right words. 'I'm sorry. For everything. For not telling you earlier, for hurting you.'

'It doesn't matter any more,' Antoine said. 'It's in the past. We've all changed. And I'm glad you're both happy—and that you have the little one.'

Her eyes filled with tears. 'Thank you.'

'This is my colleague, Geri,' Antoine said. 'She's on secondment in Paris from our twinned zoo in Cambridge.'

Colleague. The word felt like a paper-cut, even though she knew it was sensible. They'd agreed to keep their relationship to themselves, after all. And introducing her to his ex as his girlfriend would be awkward. But at the same time she wished it could be more than this.

'*Bienvenue*, Geri,' Céline said. 'Are you enjoying Paris?'

'Very much,' Geri said. 'We brought a little something for you both, and for Maya.'

'Oh, this book is so lovely. Thank you so much. See, Maya? *Les animaux*.' She turned one of the pages and smiled. '*Le tigre*. Of course. Bianca.'

'Thank you, Geri. Come and sit down,' Jean-Luc said.

Céline handed the baby and the fabric book to him. 'I'll make coffee,' she said, 'and put these beautiful flowers in water.'

'Can I help?' Geri asked; apart from being polite, she had a feeling that Antoine and Jean-Luc might need a moment to themselves.

'Thank you. That would be kind.' Céline led her through to the kitchen, and put the flowers in water before putting the kettle on; she'd already shaken grounds into the cafetière and put cups and saucers on a tray, clearly prepared for the visit.

'Are you Ant's girlfriend?' Céline asked.

It was blunt, and Geri knew she and Ant

should've expected this and discussed her response. Caught off guard, she resorted to the facts. 'I'm his colleague, here on secondment. There was a problem with my flat, and I ended up staying with him.'

'I see.'

Geri could feel the heat rising in her face and knew it was giving her away. 'He was a bit prickly to start with, but we work well together and I think we've become good friends. He's helping me tick off my list of things I want to see in Paris, and also find the best place for crème brûlée for when my sister visits.'

'He said you helped him find the *doudou plat* and the tiger for the baby.'

Geri smiled. 'Yes. We had a squabble in the shop and had to toss a coin. If I'd had my way he would've sent you a panda—the pandas are why I came to Paris, to work on the breeding programme. I've loved pandas ever since I was tiny.'

Céline nodded and gave her an assessing look. 'I assume he's told you everything?'

'About the situation? Yes.'

'I never wanted to hurt him,' Céline said softly. 'Neither did Jean-Luc. I loved Ant. But when Jean-Luc came to Paris and I met him for the first time, it was like fireworks going off in my head. Like nothing I'd ever felt before. I tried to fight it—and I was never unfaithful to Ant. I thought as long as Jean-Luc wasn't in Paris, I could ignore my feelings and be the partner Ant deserved.'

'I'm not judging you,' Geri said. 'You can't help who you fall in love with.'

Céline gave a sad smile. 'But we handled it badly and we hurt Ant. I don't think either of us will ever be able to forgive ourselves for it.'

'I think he's come to terms with things,' Geri said. 'I know he misses Jean-Luc—and you. The baby was the catalyst for him to make contact with you both again.'

'I think,' Céline said, 'he would still have kept his distance, if not for you.'

'Maybe,' Geri said.

Céline gave her a hug. 'Thank you for whatever you said to him. The times Jean-Luc has wanted to call him, but it felt as if we'd be rubbing our happiness in his face and that wasn't fair. We knew we had to wait until he was ready to contact us—on his terms.'

'Ant said Jean-Luc has been texting him.'

Céline nodded. 'He says he feels as if the family can come together again. We both know it's our fault that the split happened.'

'Ant thinks it's his fault.'

Céline shook her head. 'If I hadn't called off the wedding…'

'Then you would both have been unhappy,' Geri said. 'You spared him that.'

'I wish there'd been a way to do it so nobody got hurt,' Céline said. 'And I hope we will become friends.'

'I'd like that,' Geri said.

When they took the coffee through, Ant was sitting on the sofa, holding the baby. Geri's heart squeezed. Right at that moment, she could imagine him holding his own child. It made her wonder if it would be better to go back to being purely colleagues and friends; Ant was clearly a born father, and having children might be complicated for her. He'd already been hurt. How could she potentially put him through the anguish of losing a baby, or not being able to have children?

Or maybe he saw her as his transition person, and thought he was doing the same for her.

So she smiled. A lot. Even though her heart squeezed even more when it was her turn to cuddle the baby; the warmth, the weight and the little sleepy snuffles Maya gave when she fell asleep all made her think of what she'd lost. Of what might never be.

Jean-Luc insisted that they stay for lunch, and gradually Geri found herself relaxing.

'Thank you for coming to see us,' he said, kissing her cheeks, when they finally left. 'It's been good to get to know you.'

Céline followed it up with a hug. 'Thank you for bringing Ant back to us. And maybe we can come to see you in Paris.'

'I think we'd both like that,' Geri said, hugging her back.

Antoine was quiet as they walked round Chartres; but once they were in the cathedral grounds, he took her in his arms and held her close. 'Thank you,' he said. 'For giving me perspective. For persuading me to bridge that gap when I was being stubborn.'

'My pleasure. They're lovely. As is the baby.'

'I saw your face when you held her. It hurt,' he said softly.

'It did,' she admitted. 'But at the same time I think it was good for me to have close contact with a baby.'

'We're healing,' he said. 'It's going to get better.'

It was, particularly when Antoine did another ultrasound on Zhen later the following week and this time they got to see the foetus.

'Look—there's a spine,' he said, 'and the

foetus is kicking. It's about four centimetres long; I'd say we'll have a panda cub at some time in the next couple of weeks. We'll need a rota to be on panda watch in about ten days' time.'

Between work and exploring Paris with Antoine—and waking up in his arms every morning—Geri couldn't have been happier. Maybe she was storing up trouble for herself in the future, but for now she was enjoying the moment and not having to go into issues that she'd find hard to face. It would be easy to let herself love this man, but she didn't want to saddle him with the burden of her infertility. And maybe their affair would come to a natural end when her placement was over. So she was just going to enjoy her time with him and ignore the shadows.

She managed that until the day the lab gave them the bad news about Bianca's bloods.

'Her kidneys have deteriorated a lot more since the last tests,' Antoine said. 'I can't give her any meds to make things better. I know they've had success with kidney transfers in cats, but I don't know of any in tigers— and even if a kidney was available from another tiger and we could do some pioneering surgery, there's no guarantee the transplant would work or give her a better quality of life.' He took a deep breath. 'I can't let her suffer. I need to speak to the directors; they need to ratify my clinical decision.'

She knew the decision he meant. The one that all vets hated having to make. 'Do you want me to go with you? For moral support, I mean?' she asked.

'No. But I think Belle could do with a hug,' he said. 'I'll come and find you when I've spoken to the directors.'

When he came to find them, he was grim-faced. 'It's agreed. We need to say goodbye.'

'She came to the zoo the same day you did,' Belle said. 'A year before I joined.'

He nodded. 'This will be hard. But we need to do it, for her sake.'

Belle's eyes filled with tears. 'I know.' She called Bianca, who came padding over to the bars where they stood and made a soft chuffing noise.

'My lovely girl,' she said. 'It's going to be hard, not having you saying hello to me every day.'

The tiger chuffed at her.

'We've been here together since that first day,' Antoine said. 'I can't imagine the zoo without you. But we need to let you run free and be out of pain.'

'Down, girl,' Belle whispered; as Bianca lay down, she gave the tiger a treat.

Antoine had already prepared the syringe. 'Good girl,' he said, and Belle gave her another treat.

'I know you're tired, my lovely. So tired. And we'll miss you very, very much. But now it's time for you to sleep,' Antoine said.

The tiger made a soft chuff as if to say goodbye.

Belle was shaking with the effort of not sobbing out loud and distressing the tiger, and Geri slid an arm round her shoulders.

Antoine knelt next to the tiger. '*Poussée*, Bianca,' he said and slowly eased the tip of the syringe into her vein. This time, Geri wasn't on intubation duties, because this time the tiger wasn't going to wake up, and she had a lump in her throat.

'Run free, *ma petite*,' Antoine said, and stroked the tiger's flank before withdrawing his hand and the syringe.

His eyes were wet, and now Belle was sobbing openly.

Geri put her arms round both of them, trying to comfort them as best she could.

She wasn't sure how any of them got through the day. Antoine did his rounds while avoiding everyone as much as possible; Belle had the other tigers to look after, but was clearly hurting; and Geri was worried about Antoine.

The only thing she could think of to do was the same thing that he'd done for her. She popped out to the nearest shops and bought flowers; then found him in his office at the end of the day.

'Come on,' she said gently. 'You need to get out of here.'

'I just…the world feels flat,' he said. 'And I know it's ridiculous, being this upset about a tiger.'

'A tiger who joined the zoo the same day that you did. A tiger who knew your voice and came and chuffed at you, as if you were one of her pack. That's not any old tiger,' she said. 'Come with me.'

'Forgive me, Geri, but I'm not in the mood for exploring Paris tonight.'

'We're not exploring,' she said. 'I have petals.'

His eyes glittered in recognition of what she meant. 'That's…'

'You don't have to speak,' she said. 'I know.'

With the help of the map on her phone, she took him to the Parc Monceau and found the

Venetian bridge. 'I thought here might be a nice spot to remember her,' she said.

'Very nice.' He took a handful of flower petals and scattered them on the water. 'Vets aren't supposed to have favourites.'

'In theory, but we all do. My best friend at my old practice has a jar of dog treats in her consulting room, and any springer spaniels coming in for a check-up or inoculations or investigations get an extra bit of fuss.'

The anecdote made him smile, as she'd hoped it would.

'I connected with Bianca,' he said. 'My apartment isn't suitable for keeping a dog, but maybe I should get a cat.'

'A black and white one,' she suggested.

'Called Bianca,' he said. 'Though I think you'd name a black and white cat "Panda".'

'It's a great name for a cat. Short for Pandemonium,' she said. 'Which is what all the best kittens will cause.'

'Yeah.' His voice thickened, and he sprinkled more petals onto the water below. 'Or maybe I could adopt a rescue cat.'

'Maybe,' she said with a smile.

He sprinkled the rest of the petals in silence, and she knew in his head he was saying goodbye to the white tigress who'd been there for his whole time at the zoo. And it would hurt as much as saying goodbye to a beloved pet.

He didn't say much on the way back to his apartment, though when she reached for his hand his fingers tightened round hers. When she offered to cook them both dinner, he shook his head. 'I'm not hungry.'

She stroked his face. 'I would offer to make you a mug cake, but you hated the last one.'

'I appreciated the kindness,' he said.

'I'm going to make an omelette,' she said. 'Which won't be anything like a proper Parisian one, but you're welcome to share it. Even if you only take one mouthful.'

He slid his arms round her and held her close. 'You're one of a kind, Geri Milligan. A very special kind. And you make the world a better place just by being in it.'

She caught her breath. 'I think that's the nicest thing anyone's ever said to me.'

'It's true,' he said, drawing back to look her in the eye. 'You've changed my world. You've brought me out of the dark little shell I was hiding in. You've helped me to start rebuilding my relationship with my brother. You've helped me to open up to my colleagues at the zoo again—even Sylvie with her relentless barrage of terrible jokes.'

'You would've got there yourself in the end,' she said.

He shook his head. 'It's more than that. You've reminded me that the world is full of sunshine. In Monet's garden, you taught me to see spring flowers like his paintings. You've made me remember how much I love Paris, from the little hidden corners right through to the Eiffel Tower sparkling at night. And even today, when my heart's sore and I'm out of sorts, you're like this warm light welcoming me home.' He drew his hand up to her mouth. 'Over the last few weeks, I've come to realise that I love you. And I know what we said about there being all sorts of reasons why we shouldn't do this—but there's a bigger reason why we should. Why we can work things out between us. Will you stay with me in Paris and maybe make a family with me, Geri?'

Stay with him.

Make a family with him.

But what if she couldn't? What if the Q fever had caused irreversible damage and they couldn't have children? What if all the strains of miscarriages and IVF treatment ripped them apart?

Panic flooded through her.

She liked Ant. More than liked him. If she

was honest with herself, she'd fallen in love with the quiet, formal Parisian with his hidden depths. Kissing him beneath the spring blossom made her pulse beat faster and filled her head with starlight.

But.

He'd been badly hurt by Céline not being honest with him. Geri knew Ant wanted children; so did she, but that was something she couldn't guarantee.

It would be fairer to walk away. Give him the chance to meet someone else, someone who could share his dreams without complications.

'I can't,' she whispered. 'I'm so sorry. I *can't.*'

He stared at her, looking shocked. 'But—I thought you felt the same way I did.'

She did.

Which was what made this so very hard.

If she talked it through with him, he'd make everything sound reasonable. But how could she be sure they'd be able to overcome the obstacles? She'd loved Mark and their marriage had worked—until they'd lost the baby and discovered there was such a huge gulf between their hopes and dreams. Their marriage had failed because they both wanted different things; but her relationship with Antoine could fail because they both wanted the same things—and it might not happen.

And she couldn't risk going through that.

'I can't,' she said. 'I'm not perfect and I can't do this to you. I just can't.'

'But, Geri—'

'I can't,' she said. Overwhelmed by misery and needing space, she rushed out of the room in tears.

CHAPTER TEN

IT WAS JUST as well she'd only brought one suitcase to Paris, Geri thought, because it meant it was a lot easier for her to pack. To move into a hotel that night—because it really wasn't fair to keep staying with Antoine when she'd turned down his proposal. To find a flat in the next couple of days: a tiny apartment in an Art Deco building in the sixteenth arrondissement, a beautiful building full of curves, with pale cream bricks and its tall windows, shutters and balconies painted pale green.

Her flat wasn't far from the Eiffel Tower, and she got to see the sparkles every single night. If she'd found the place during her first week in Paris, she would've loved living here; but, although the apartment was much smaller than Antoine's spacious duplex, it felt echoey and empty. She'd grown used to sharing breakfast with him, asking if he wanted a drink before she put the kettle on—or having him surprise her with a cup of tea, precisely the way she liked it. Cooking dinner with him, if they weren't going out exploring Paris. Curled up on the sofa together, reading. All the little things of a shared life added up to much more than the whole.

Travelling to the zoo was strange, too: on her own rather than having Antoine to chat to and to point out things, and having to remember to catch a different train and change lines halfway through the journey. And work was excruciating. Antoine was cool and professional with her, and he'd gone back to eating lunch at his desk rather than joining the team; she was guiltily aware that he was slipping back into his old isolation, and she knew it was her fault. Everyone seemed aware that something had happened between them: but nobody asked. An invisible barrier had gone up, and Geri no longer felt part of the team; she was a stranger in a strange land. All she could do was simply do her job to the best of her ability.

And it was all her own fault that she felt utterly miserable. She'd panicked and pushed Antoine away—and, in the process, she'd hurt him and broken her own heart. Worse, she'd hurt him on a day when he'd already been vulnerable. She'd never be able to forgive herself for that.

'You look terrible,' Sally Milligan said. 'I'm getting on the next train to Paris.'

'Mum, no. You've got work tomorrow,' Geri protested.

'My daughter's more important,' Sally said, 'and anyway I can work extra hours next week, to catch up.'

'Mum, I love you, but you really don't have to rush over here,' Geri said.

'I know something's up, because your texts stopped being sparkly,' Sally said. 'What's happened?'

Geri gave in and told her mother the whole sorry story.

'It sounds to me,' Sally said, 'as if you haven't given him a choice.'

'He's been hurt before. I don't want to put him through having a proper relationship with me, only to find I can't give him the family he wants.'

'Apart from the fact that you have other options, such as fostering or adoption,' Sally said, 'he wants the same things that you do. It's not like it was with Mark. If he loves you, and you love him, you'll find a way to sort things out—*together*.'

'But that's the point, Mum. How do I know he really loves me? How do I know he didn't just ask me to stay because he was trying to make himself feel better after his favourite tiger died?'

'You don't. So talk to him,' Sally said. 'Be honest.'

But Geri couldn't find the words. Even Zhen giving birth to a tiny nine-hundred-gram cub didn't raise her spirits. Geri had been looking forward to seeing a newborn panda and watching it grow, seeing the white fur start to cover its pink skin over the first couple of days, followed swiftly by the black markings around its eyes and on its body. She should've been thrilled by its loud squeals when it wanted to nurse or for Zhen to reposition it, knowing that regular loud squeaks were signs of a healthy cub. And even taking part in the first assessment of the cub—checking its heartbeat and lung sounds, checking the umbilicus, palpating the abdomen—didn't delight her as much as it should've done. Antoine didn't seem as excited and thrilled about the cub as she'd expected, either; though, given how much she'd hurt him, she wasn't surprised that he'd gone all detached.

Guilt at how much pain she'd caused him, and misery at how much she'd wrecked everything between them, spoiled everything.

Geri definitely wasn't herself, Ant thought. She'd always been professional at work, but she'd been bubbly too, full of enthusiasm. He'd been prepared for her to watch the cub-cam every minute of the day on her phone when she wasn't at work, in case she saw a glimpse of the cub, and to tell him snippets of facts she'd learned—how quickly panda cubs grew, how their eyes didn't open until eight weeks and that for the first two weeks they couldn't urinate or defecate unless their mum licked them to stimulate them. How panda dads were incredibly hands off and never actually had anything to do with their cubs.

Instead, she was quiet at work. The sparkle had gone from her eyes.

The sparkle had gone from his life, too. The apartment felt hideously empty without her. And everywhere he looked, there were lovers holding hands, kissing, sharing a smile, enjoying the city.

He missed doing that with Geri.

He missed *her.*

Did she miss him as much as he missed her? Was that why she was quiet and cool and professional instead of *le petit rayon* he'd teased her about being?

Maybe he should ask her. Get her to really talk to him. Persuade her to tell him why she'd backed off, when he'd been sure they felt the same way—and then work out how to overcome every single barrier she'd put up. She'd taught him something important after he'd let the gulf between him and Jean-Luc grow instead of trying to bridge it; he knew if he repeated that mistake with Geri, she'd go back to England and he'd lose her for good.

He knew he'd pushed her too far, too fast. Now, he needed to let her know that he'd wait until she was ready. That he was prepared to work at this. But, to do that, he had to get her to talk to him. How?

He knew she loved romcoms, because he'd overheard her talking about movies to Belle and Valerie. Maybe there was something he could do connected to a film. Something she wouldn't expect him to do, and it would make her lower her guard.

An hour's browsing on the internet decided him.

That evening, he headed towards the building where she lived. Throwing stones at a window was a bad idea; but he could throw roses. Particularly as she was only on the first floor; and, even better, it looked as if she'd opened her window to let the heat out of the room.

Everything was cued up on his phone, and he had one earphone in to help him keep vaguely in tune.

Ignoring the curious glances of passers-by, he threw the first rose in through her window.

Geri heard a soft thud, and looked up from the French text she was reading. Rostand's *Cyrano de Bergerac*, even though the balcony scene made her throat feel scratchy with un-shed tears because she remembered Antoine telling her about it, and she *missed* him.

A second thud.

She saw the rose coming in through the window just before she heard the third soft thud as it hit the wooden flooring.

Who on earth was throwing roses through her window? Was this some kind of Parisian publicity stunt?

Frowning, she put the book down and crossed over to the window.

Red rose number four came hurtling her way, and she caught it before looking out to see who'd thrown it.

Antoine was waiting beneath the window, and he gave her a slow, slow smile. One that made her heart miss several beats.

Then, to her shock, he held the remaining roses up to her, almost as a toast, and began to sing.

She'd never heard him sing before, but his voice was beautiful. And the song he was singing gave her goosebumps. Classic Charles Aznavour—'She'—but it sounded more like the Elvis Costello version from one of her favourite films. And Antoine was singing in English rather than in French.

People were gathering in a semicircle around him, but he ignored them; he was entirely focused on her, singing his heart out to her.

She blinked back the tears as she listened to him sing. Antoine Bouvier was the last person she would've expected to make a public declaration like this—particularly as she'd already turned him down—and it made her knees weak. That smile, those intense looks, the way he sang the words as if every single one burst from his heart...

He finished singing, and all the onlookers clapped and cheered.

'*Je t'aime, mon petit rayon,*' he called. '*Je t'aime.*'

I love you.

The crowd fell silent, clearly as eager for her answer as he was.

And her throat felt clogged with tears, to the point that she couldn't speak. Instead, she gestured to him to come up.

A few moments later, her intercom buzzed. She pressed the button to release the door, and then he was there at her doorway.

'Ant... I...'

'I know.' He enfolded her in his arms.

For a long time they stood there, simply holding each other, not talking.

Then she pulled back to look him in the eye. 'I'm so sorry I hurt you.'

'It's my fault. I know I rushed you,' he said. 'And I'm probably rushing you now—but I can't help myself. I don't want you to leave, Geri. I want to be with you. I want to make a family with you.'

'But that's the point,' she said. 'You know about the Q fever. I might not be able to have children. What if I can't give you the family you want?'

'Then we adopt,' he said. 'Or foster. Or be extra "parents" to the zoo babies. There are all kinds of families. We'll make ours the best we can.'

She didn't doubt his sincerity, but it wasn't

enough to allay her fears. 'I've been married before, Ant. It went wrong, when Mark and I realised that we didn't want the same things. And the end of my marriage ripped me apart. I can't face going through that again.'

'Let's talk about this. Find out what we both want, where we can compromise, and how we can make it work,' he said. 'Sit. I'll make you a cup of tea, and we'll talk.' He groaned when he walked into her kitchen and opened the cupboard door above the kettle. 'Instant coffee?' He gave a theatrical sigh. 'What a shame. Well, as it's you, I'll manage.'

'You're such a coffee snob,' she said, relieved that he'd lightened the atmosphere.

'This is Paris,' he reminded her with a smile. 'We're all coffee snobs here. Apart from weird English zoo vets, it seems.'

He walked back into her living room, carrying two mugs, and handed one to her. 'Where do we start?'

'I don't know.'

'Telling me how you feel about me would be a good place,' he said. 'Given that I just sang my heart out to you, in front of a crowd of strangers, you already know how I feel about you.'

'If anyone had told me you'd sing up to my

balcony, I would never have believed them,' she said. 'And I love that film.'

'The actress and the bookshop guy had to overcome a lot of differences to be together,' he said.

'You've seen the film?'

He wrinkled his nose. 'I read the synopsis. Their lives were very different: she was a famous film star, while he was an ordinary guy who worked in a bookshop. There was an ocean between their countries—a bigger one than the English Channel. But they believed in love enough to give each other a chance.'

And there was the iconic bit where Julia Roberts asked Hugh Grant to love her. Which was kind of what Antoine had done to her, except he'd sung it. Such a private man, baring his heart to her in front of everyone—it was a huge, huge deal. And if he could do something that was so far from his natural way of doing things, just for her, then it gave her hope that maybe they could make this work.

'I love you, Ant,' she said.

'Good,' he said drily, 'because I've been a little concerned about that.'

With good reason. She'd hurt him. 'I'm

sorry I pushed you away.' She bit her lip. 'I guess I panicked.'

'My timing was way off,' he acknowledged. 'I should have taken it more slowly. Prepared you. Talked more about how I felt, so you knew what was in my heart before I offered it to you.'

Instead, she'd stamped on it.

'But I was…' He searched for words. 'In a dark place, I suppose, and I wanted the sunlight.'

'So you did ask me to stay with you, just to make yourself feel better.'

'Is that what you thought? Is that why you turned me down?' He shook his head. 'It was more than that. Specifically, I wanted the sunlight you've brought into my life. I wanted *you*.'

'Is that past tense?' she asked warily.

'*Mon petit rayon*, I sang the most romantic song I know to you, in English,' he pointed out. 'You can't possibly have misunderstood the message.'

She smiled wryly. 'Even little rays of sunshine get paranoid.'

'I love you, Geri,' he said. 'And I want to be with you. I want to make a family with you. I know it's not going to be easy, and I'm prepared for that. If you can't have children, there are other options we can explore.'

Her heart skipped a beat. Could it be true?

'What about all our other differences?' she asked. 'For a start, you live in Paris and I live in England.'

'It's a little too far to commute,' he acknowledged. 'But one of us could move. We can toss a coin for it. Or we could spend half the year in Paris and half the year in Cambridge. Our zoos are part of the same organisation; we'll simply ask them to accommodate us.'

'And if they can't?'

'Then we consider doing consultancy work,' he said.

'Freelance.' Financially, that'd be precarious.

As if her worries showed on her face, he said, 'If you're worrying about a salary and how we'll manage, it's not an issue. I don't have a mortgage.' He looked away. 'I, um, own the rest of my building, too. I rent the other three apartments to tenants.'

He owned a whole building in an upmarket part of Paris? That meant he was a lot wealthier than she'd thought. And that threw up another barrier. 'I, um… What if your family thinks I'm a gold-digger?'

'My family,' he said, 'will think nothing of the kind. You've already met Jean-Luc, and he likes you very much. I've told my sister and my parents about you, and they're dying to meet you.' He looked at her. 'How will your family react to me?'

'I've talked to them a lot about you,' she said. 'They already like the sound of you. When they meet you, they'll love you. And that's a definite.'

'Good. Next obstacle?' he asked, clearly intent on finding every single one and dealing with it.

'I…' She blew out a breath. 'This whole thing about us being colleagues—it's not really an issue, is it?'

'No,' he said.

'What about your obstacles?' she asked.

'I don't have any,' he said. 'Because I want the same things that you do. To love you for the rest of my days, to make a family with you, and to work with you in a job I love. Where we live and work don't actually matter. We can live anywhere you like—as long as we're together.'

He'd do that for her? Move from Paris? Hope began to flare in the deep hollow space she'd thought would stay empty for ever.

She put her hand to his cheek. 'But you love Paris, Ant.'

'I admit I've fallen back in love with my home city, thanks to you,' he said. 'But Paris won't be enough for me if you're not here. For me, home is where you are. If that's England, then it's England.'

She could see in his eyes that he meant it.

'I know we have differences,' he said. 'The way you drink tea is appalling. And your mug cakes make an utter mess of the microwave.'

'You're way too fussy about the way cheese should be cut—and served,' she retorted. 'Crackers are one of life's joys.'

'Good bread,' he said, 'is better.' He grinned. 'Our differences will make life more interesting. I *like* bickering with you. And we can always toss a coin if we can't agree—like we did in the shop.'

'Our nursery will be themed with pandas,' she said.

'Our nursery will have tigers,' he corrected. 'And we'll have that mobile you liked. The one with the clouds and the sun and the rainbow.'

'That's us. You all brooding clouds, me all sunshine.' The flicker of hope was becoming a steady flame now, growing brighter. 'And together we'll make rainbows.'

'The mobile had fluffy clouds, not brooding,' he said. 'Perhaps you can teach me to be fluffy.'

She grinned. 'Docteur le Nuage… What's French for fluffy?'

He grinned back. *'Duveteux.'*

'No way! You're making that up,' she accused.

'No, really it is. Look it up. Or *pelucheux* might be better,' he mused.

'Docteur le Nuage Pelucheux,' she said.

He groaned. 'Please don't call me that at work.'

She laughed. 'I wouldn't be that mean.'

'You'd better not be. Any more obstacles?'

There was the big one. 'Ant, I… I love you, and I love the way you understand me, and the way you made my dark day of the year bearable for the first time since it happened. You make me feel brave—and with you I don't have to fake it any more.'

'Good,' he said. 'Though I can see there's another "but".'

She held him more tightly. 'What if I can't have children? What if the Q fever comes back?'

'Then we'll deal with it,' he said. 'And we'll deal with it *together.*' He stroked her face. 'As I said before, we have options. Maybe we could think about adoption or fostering. And you have my backing, always.'

She could see the sincerity in his eyes.

'So is there anything else worrying you?' he asked.

Geri scrubbed the threatening tears away with the back of her hand. 'With you by my side, I can face anything.' She took a deep breath. 'I know it's a lot to ask, that I've made you jump through hoops.'

His eyes narrowed. 'But?'

She stroked his face. 'Antoine Bouvier, I want to learn French poetry and how to cut cheese the way you like it. Will you live with me and be my love?'

'Yes,' he said. And then he dropped to one knee. 'Though I want more than that. I don't have a ring, but I'd rather choose it with you in any case. Geri Milligan, will you marry me and make a family with me?'

'Yes,' she said. 'Though we need to seal the deal.'

'I think we might agree on how we do that,' he said, rising to his feet, and kissed her.

There was only one answer to that. She smiled. *D'accord.*

EPILOGUE

Two years later

GERI WALKED HAND in hand through the Zoo de Bélvèdere with her husband, their six-week-old daughter strapped into the sling on his chest.

'Louise, here are the pandas. This is why your *maman* came to France,' she said.

The baby gurgled.

'Though she stayed for your *papa*,' Antoine said.

'Because I fell in love with pandas, with Paris, and with your *papa*. Not in that order,' Geri said with a smile.

'I should hope not, Dr Bouvier,' Antoine said reprovingly, though his eyes were full of laughter. 'It's been an amazing two years.'

'The anniversary of the day you threw roses in my window and proposed to me,' she said.

'We'll have champagne tonight,' he said.

'I thought the French were fussy and insisted on rosé for their barbecues?' she asked.

He laughed. 'The barbecue's tomorrow night. Our parents are babysitting tonight.'

Since they'd moved to a house in the fifteenth arrondissement—in a leafy street, with a sunny living area—Antoine's parents had moved into his old apartment, and his sister had taken over the vineyard completely. Her parents and sister visited often, and their living room and kitchen were usually filled with family and friends. Including Jean-Luc and Céline, whose second baby was due in a month; Geri and Céline had become firm friends. Along with a black and white cat called Bianca and a dog of undetermined parentage called Blue, they'd made the family Geri had dreamed of.

'Babysitting, hmm?' She gave him a sidelong look. 'What did you have in mind?'

'I was planning,' he said, 'to take my beautiful wife for dinner, on a rooftop terrace with a good view of the Eiffel Tower.'

'And dancing?' she asked.

'Oh, I guarantee there will be dancing,' he murmured in her ear, his voice low and husky.

Desire shimmered through her. 'Perfect. *Je t'aime*, Dr Bouvier.'

'And I love you too, Dr Bouvier,' he said.

* * * * *

*If you enjoyed this story, check out
these other great reads from
Kate Hardy*

Saving Christmas for the ER Doc
Surgeon's Second Chance in Florence
Baby Miracle for the ER Doc
Second Chance with Her Guarded GP

All available now!